Unfortunate Death *of* Lord Longbottom

*

The Lady Jane & Mrs Forbes Mysteries

Book Four

B. D. CHURSTON

This is a work of fiction. All names, characters, locations and incidents are products of the author's imagination, or have been used fictitiously. Any resemblance to actual persons living or dead, locales, or events is entirely coincidental. No part of this book may be reproduced without prior written permission from the author.

Copyright © 2024 B. D. CHURSTON

All rights reserved.

ISBN: 9798332877308

One

October 1928

Lady Jane Scott, the twenty-seven-year-old daughter of the Earl of Oxley, examined the invitation card tucked behind an ornate silver candlestick on Kate Forbes' front room mantlepiece.

"A big night tonight, Aunt."

A quick glance told Kate that her niece was studying Lord Longbottom's invitation to an event at Sandham Town Hall that evening.

"Yes," she acknowledged, "but right now, I can only think about lunch, Jane. They'll wonder where we've got to."

Having broken a two-inch patent leather heel in the street a few minutes earlier, Kate was perched on the edge of the sofa changing her footwear.

"Are you sure you don't want me to come along tonight, Aunt?"

"No, honestly, you'd find it deathly dull. Thanks all the same."

The event had been set up to discuss how the town might attract more summertime visitors. That would mean three hours of listening to daft ideas while quaffing cheap sherry and munching on bland sandwiches cut into quarters.

"I'll head back to London after lunch then… if that's alright?"

"Of course it is. Go out and enjoy yourself tonight."

"Alright, you've talked me into it."

Kate smiled. To think that up to a mere ten months ago, she and Jane had spent years drifting apart almost to the point of becoming strangers. The incident at Linton Hall last December changed all that, of course.

And since then?

Kate wouldn't have chosen murder, mayhem and tangling with Inspector Ridley of Scotland Yard as a way to bond with her niece, but there was no point complaining about it. Anyway, the mayhem was behind them now. Life was ordinary once more and their biggest concern was being late for a social engagement.

"Right!" she said, getting to her feet. "Let's try again, shall we?"

For the second time in fifteen minutes, the duo set out under a blue October sky for a Wednesday lunch date at the Crown Hotel, although this time with a little more urgency as they made their way down Cobb Lane and across the High Street.

"Hey, what's the rush!" demanded renowned local curmudgeon, Ernie Melton as they overtook him at the top of Royal Avenue.

"We're training for the next Olympics," wheezed Kate as they left him in their wake – although she doubted any international sprinter did their training in a heavy tweed, dark orange twinset.

A short way ahead, on the western corner of Royal Avenue and the Promenade, stood Sandham-on-Sea's largest building: the six-storey, seventy-room Crown Hotel – its French Renaissance Revival edifice having dominated the locale since 1888. It overlooked the beach and the English Channel, where seventy miles to the south, lay France and the Continent of Europe.

"At last," gasped Kate as she and Jane burst into its cavernous oak-panelled lobby, where countless guests had no doubt admired the grand staircase, two lifts, crystal chandeliers, gilt-framed mirrors, and oil paintings of various royals.

Kate called out a cheery hello to coiffed blonde-haired Sally behind the reception desk before turning to a large mirror to catch her breath and tidy her collar-length hair. As ever, there was the continuing takeover bid of her dark brown locks by the forces of grey. That said, regular walking was keeping the rest of her in pretty good shape at fifty-three.

She glanced at the reflection of her niece beside her. The auburn hair tucked stylishly behind her ears… those warm brown eyes… the friendly smile… it all belied a mind as sharp and meticulous as any Kate had ever known.

"Right then, Jane. Shall we…?"

The duo pushed through the double doors to the half-full, thirty-table dining room — a space decorated in the classical style to such an obvious degree, it was practically thumbing its nose at the plain, angular designs being promoted more and more by fashionable magazines.

Kate immediately spotted Pru Davenport wearing a pink blouse under a mauve blazer, and Ginny Howard in a sea-green tweed twinset and pearl necklace.

"Pru, Ginny!" she called prior to joining them.

"We were about to send out a search party," said Lady Davenport – Pru to her friends. "Jane, as always, you look as fresh as a daisy. Kate, you look as if you've been pulling a wagon."

"I had a heel give way no sooner we left the house. Blow me down if my other good shoes didn't match my outfit."

"Well, you're here now," said Ginny Howard, the doctor's wife. "That's what matters."

"Absolutely," said Kate.

This was to be a farewell lunch before Ginny went off for a week's stay with her sister in Chichester. Hardly a trip around the world, but the three elder ladies didn't need an excuse to swap their regular midweek lunch at Pru's for a proper pampering at the Crown. Indeed, they had already booked a 'Welcome Home, Ginny' lunch for the following Wednesday.

"So, Jane," prompted Pru, "how are things?"

"Great, thanks."

"And how is Harry?"

Pru held a firm view on Jane and Harry. Seeing as both were Oxford University historians with an interest in the same periods – the Normans through to the Elizabethans – surely it was a perfect match.

Jane took it in her stride though.

"He's in London contemplating the early impact of the Norman Conquest on our remote communities. Right now, he's probably staring into space in the British Library."

"Staring into space?" said Pru. "No doubt, thinking of you and pining like a lost puppy. Still, he'll see you soon enough."

Jane smiled. She had only been away two days and she'd be catching the train home in a couple of hours.

"And what of you, Kate?" asked Pru. "Speaking of researchers, how are things with Professor Nash?"

"He's working on something at a library in Oxford."

"I wonder if *he's* pining?" said Ginny.

"Professors don't pine," said Kate, although now she was wondering about that.

"We have the utmost respect for widowhood and a period of mourning," said Pru, "but there's also your future to consider."

Kate thought of her dear-departed husband, Henry. He would have probably agreed with Pru, but that didn't mean standards should be cast aside.

"Nothing's changed between the professor and me since you asked last week. We're on friendly terms, that's all."

"Really? How does he address you in his correspondence?"

"That's private."

"You're among friends."

Kate picked up her menu.

"If you must know, he addresses me as Dear Kate, and he signs off with fondest regards, Perry."

"He's not the florid type then?"

"He's a professor of history, Pru, not a romance author."

Jane failed to hide a smirk, but Pru wasn't finished.

"How do you reply to him, Kate? Please don't say, Dear Professor Nash."

Jane's smirk turned into suppressed laughter.

"I can't think why it's of interest," said Kate, "but I use Dear Perry and sign off Yours Sincerely, Kate."

"Have you thought of spicing things up," suggested Ginny.

"Ginny, really!" admonished Kate. She then wondered about it. "How would I spice things up?"

"Address him as Dearest Perry. That'll have him in a lather when he reads it."

Kate decided that things were getting a little out of hand.

"I know it's 1928, ladies, and that attitudes are getting quite modern…"

Pru waved the protest away.

"Honestly, from what Jane tells me, you and Perry are made for each other."

Kate's eyebrows shot up.

"Jane told you…?"

Jane slunk down a little. "Sorry, Aunt. It was when I popped down to see you a couple of weeks ago. We bumped into Lady Davenport. Do you remember?"

"Of course I remember. I only left you two alone for a minute."

Jane shrugged. "It was long enough for her to force it out of me."

Kate put her menu down.

"Alright… I've only known the professor since we met at Penford Priory six weeks ago. Despite the horrible business Jane and I had to deal with there, I found Perry's company quite something. I never imagined meeting another man after Henry… and I don't want to rush things. We've only met once since and have corresponded half a dozen times."

"Jane says he's a thoroughly decent widower," said Pru.

"He's also dedicated to his work, and rightly so," said Kate. "And if you must know, he's coming to Sandham on Saturday. We'll be having lunch right here."

"Oh marvellous!" said Pru. "I was thinking of popping in for lunch on Saturday too."

"No, you weren't," said Kate.

"If you say so."

Ginny looked disappointed. "I'll be in boring Chichester."

"Don't be too down in the dumps," said Pru. "I'm sure Kate will give us a full and accurate report."

"Hmmm… speaking of being down in the dumps," said Kate. "Have you noticed Lord Longbottom over there."

A few tables away, Lord Herbert Longbottom, a portly, balding man of around sixty in a blue three-piece flannel suit, was having lunch with Mr Swithin, the bank manager – a dour chap in his fifties with a liking for plain brown suits. Lord Longbottom looked a lot less cheery than usual. Where he would normally lead the conversation, he was noticeably withdrawn.

"He looks troubled by something," said Pru. "I wonder if it's Mr Swithin's endless fund of dull stories?"

Kate had to agree. Not about Mr Swithin but concerning Lord Longbottom. Despite being a widower of five years, he was usually the cheeriest man around. Clearly something was bothering him. If she got a chance, she would ask if she could help in any way. After all, that's what friends were for.

The ladies made their way outside, where Kate wondered if she'd get a chance to speak to Lord Longbottom. It wasn't a matter of learning what was troubling him, it was just her wanting to offer a friendly smile at a time it might be appreciated.

The first thing she noticed was his dark blue Rolls-Royce Silver Ghost parked just beyond the Davenports' green Alvis tourer – but with no sign of Herbert.

"That's odd," she muttered.

Beyond the cars, an unaccompanied Mr Swithin was scuttling his way up Royal Avenue towards the High Street, no doubt heading back to the bank.

She looked the other way.

"Ah…"

His lordship had wandered along the sunny promenade just past the tea rooms and was looking thoughtfully out to sea.

It seemed out of character.

"Ladies, if you'll give me a minute…"

She stepped onto the promenade but held back a little in the hope he might turn to face her. His gaze though remained seaward where three or four boats near the horizon glinted in the sunlight.

"Herbert?" she enquired.

Lord Longbottom turned… and smiled.

"Hello, Kate. I saw you in the dining hall, but I didn't like to disturb you and the ladies."

"Don't be daft, you're always welcome. It's just that right now you seem to have the weight of the world on your shoulders."

"Not the weight of the world, Kate, but nonetheless a serious matter. Extremely serious, in fact."

"Yes, well, you and Mr Swithin having lunch together is strictly none of my business."

"Oh, it's nothing to do with him. No, this is something else. I can't say anything, but I'll have a word with the person in question this evening."

Kate knew that 'having a word' was Herbert Longbottom's preferred way. He wasn't the confrontational type.

"Well, hopefully, you'll also get to enjoy discussing ideas. I'm looking forward to drumming up support for my visitor information office suggestion. When I say support, I mean money, obviously."

"I'm sure you'll do well. In you, this town has a very fine champion."

Kate hoped she wasn't blushing.

"That's very kind."

"Think back to the Bank Holiday. We want all those people to return and spend more time here."

"Yes, we do."

The beach was quiet now, but on the August Bank Holiday, that day off work for most, the crowds had flocked to Sandham to see temporary beach stages offering concert parties to sing along with, comedians to laugh along with, Punch and Judy shows, pantomime performers, jugglers, acrobats and clowns. Had that been only a couple of months ago?

"It's important work, Kate. Keep it up."

"I will."

He smiled and she withdrew.

Yes, it had been Kate's idea to try a combined approach to improving the town's summertime economy. Her reasoning was that the Chamber of Commerce lacked breadth, the town council lacked vision, and the Women's Institute lacked power. A new, broader forum would draw from many sources, both in terms of money and ideas. At least that was the hope. Of course, she wouldn't have got far without Lord Longbottom agreeing to set up an inaugural 'We're Backing Sandham' event. Thanks to him, the first step was almost upon them. If it went well, the following step would be to set up a committee.

Waiting by the hotel, Pru, Ginny and Jane looked concerned as Kate rejoined them.

"Is he alright?" Ginny asked.

"Yes, I think so."

"Will he be at the town hall this evening?" wondered Pru.

"Yes, he will."

"Hmm," said Ginny, "I'm sure he'll be back to his usual self once he's had a glass or two of sherry."

"Exactly," said Pru.

Kate decided not to mention the serious matter on Lord Longbottom's mind. Like Ginny and Pru, her hope was that an evening among friends might lift his spirits.

"Can I give anyone a lift?" Pru asked.

"Yes, please," said Ginny.

"We're walking," said Kate, on the basis that it was hardly worth getting in and out of the car for a journey of three hundred yards.

This prompted goodbyes from Pru and Ginny to Jane, who seemed to enjoy receiving their advice regarding Harry.

Five minutes later, halfway up Cobb Lane, Kate and Jane arrived at a detached, red brick Victorian house with a small, neat front garden and a motor car parked down the side – a cherry red, two-seater Austin Seven Chummy who went by the name of Gertie.

While Jane collected her things, Kate marvelled once again at how their relationship had turned out after all the ups and downs.

It hadn't been easy. In 1919, Jane lost her mother, Annette, to Spanish flu. Annette had, of course, been Kate's talented, funny, loving younger sister. While things between aunt and niece remained strong for a time, Jane eventually went up to Somerville College, Oxford and, for a good few years, circumstances largely kept them apart. That is, until Linton Hall. Since then, Kate's main ambition had been to become the best aunt possible.

"Ready," said Jane.

They were soon in the car heading north to the edge of town. Not long after, they pulled up outside Sandham Railway Station, a small, single-storey building with a white picket fence on either side over which poked rosebushes still displaying creamy-white blooms.

"Right then," said Jane as she jumped out with her bag.

Kate got out of the car too and met her niece by the front bumper.

"Have a good journey, Jane."

"I will – and you have a successful evening."

"I will."

A hangover from the Victorian era meant that public displays of affection were still frowned upon by some. But aunt and niece didn't care too much about that and so hugged each other, causing an elderly porter to raise his eyes.

A moment later, Jane disappeared into the station, leaving Kate to wonder how long it would be before she saw her niece again.

Three

Around the middle of the 10th century, the Saxons settled in Sandham, perhaps attracted by the harbour and the prospect of not having to rely solely on agriculture to survive and thrive. Fishing therefore came to define the character of the local economy for the next 900 years.

Since the arrival of the railway in 1852 though, a wider range of economic activities had gradually taken over – not least of all, the multi-faceted business of providing for summertime visitors.

For Kate, the next step was clear – not just to attract more of them but to make them fall in love with Sandham's healthy climate, accessible beach, picturesque natural harbour and other attractions so that they might return year after year.

Hence her mission as she left her home in Cobb Lane on a mild evening – to bolster the less-than-numerous 'other' attractions on offer. To achieve this, she was attending the inaugural gathering of the 'We're Backing Sandham' campaign at the town hall, where wealth and brains would hopefully come up with ways and means.

Unfortunately, not everyone saw it as Kate did. Indeed, a fair number of the initial invitations sent out by Lord Longbottom had been politely declined by those no doubt fearing a raid on their wallets. Still, his lordship had sent out a second batch to bolster the numbers. Things would hopefully be alright.

Halfway up North Street, opposite the Alhambra Theatre, stood Sandham Town Hall. There was no competition between the two buildings for the grandest front. The theatre's four Greek doric columns against the town hall's two had long decided that argument. That said, the town hall was a slightly larger building, having similar width and depth to the Alhambra, but with the added heft of a clock tower and basement.

Kate approached the town hall entrance with her invitation at the ready. Showing it to gain entry would normally be a matter of sweeping inside without a fuss. However, the doorman was Ernie Melton, a retired chap who seemingly took on endless volunteer roles as part of a campaign to annoy as many people as possible.

Standing beside Ernie was Guy Royston, headmaster at the prestigious All Saints School for Boys. He wore his sixty years well and looked dapper in a smart grey suit. He was with his wife, Hilda, who looked resplendent in a midnight blue dress. She was busy chatting with Mrs Deane of the Coronation Dining Rooms, who wore grey. She, in turn, was with her flannel-suited husband, Mr Deane, who was waving to a burly, round-cheeked, pot-bellied chap in a dark jacket coming along the street from the other direction. It looked like local landowner-farmer Fred Brigstock, although this wasn't someone Kate knew particularly well.

"Can I see your invitation?" Ernie Melton asked as Kate came to a halt.

"I'm waving it at you," she replied.

"Yes, well, I can't read it unless you keep it still."

Guy Royston smiled apologetically to Kate, as if he were somehow party to this ludicrous charade.

"Mrs Forbes," he said, "what a pleasure to see you. And you too, Mr Brigstock."

"Evening, evening," said a genial Fred.

Kate then spotted another arrival coming along the street. This was tall, blond Robert Patterson, a thirty-year-old carpenter looking awkward in a dark blue suit. He had recently returned to Sandham, having lived and worked in Littlehampton for a few years. Kate vaguely knew his mother.

"Wonderful," she uttered. "Always happy to see new blood come into the fold."

He smiled in a friendly manner as he proudly brandished his invitation. She admired his spirit. Here was a man building up his business and reputation. He might not be ready to provide funds for Kate's visitor information office, but she would give him one of her 'the only way is up' talks – which would be apt seeing as he was a carpenter who specialised in roofs.

Meanwhile, another of Kate's targets was getting out of a royal blue Rolls-Royce Phantom and looking smart in a navy-blue blazer and crimson cravat. It was hard to think of a more self-confident, self-satisfied individual. When it came to supporting a visitor initiative, a bit of investment was needed. On that score, Desmond Ainsley had money. He also had a good eye for money-making ideas. On the downside, he'd only moved to Sandham from Worthing a couple of years ago, probably to distance himself from the people he'd upset. After all, not many folk warmed to a money lender.

"Evening all," he announced cheerily.

"Your invitation, Mr Ainsley…?" asked Ernie.

"Yes, of course, dear chap. It's on the mantlepiece at home. If you run, you'll be there and back in no time. Ask for Mrs Hibbert. She's my housekeeper. Now, stand aside. You're blocking my entry."

Ernie stood aside, muttering, "I don't know why I bother."

Kate smiled as she went in. She didn't know why he bothered either.

Four

Kate entered the capacious main hall to find thirty or so standing around nibbling tired-looking quarter-sandwiches and sipping sherry. It took a moment for her to spot Lord Herbert Longbottom in conversation with someone at the far end.

It was a lovely space, with chandelier-style electric lights, oil portraits of past mayors, a large stone fireplace, and a polished hardwood floor. Against the side wall, a line of cloth-covered tables offered more sandwiches and sherry while a waitress stood ready to assist anyone who needed help with plates or glasses.

The food Kate would leave – she'd had sausage and mash two hours earlier. Instead, she took a glass of sherry and smiled at the tall Mr Ash from the Alhambra Theatre, who was in conversation with the short Mr Boyle of the Regal Picture House and Mr Swithin, the local branch manager of the Southern Counties Bank.

"I was hoping you'd say that. It's also why I'm grateful for Lord Longbottom's invitation. It's not all take though. I'd also like to volunteer an idea I've had – if that's alright…?"

"Please, don't let me stop you."

"Well, there's no real play area for younger kids in Sandham. I know they can run amok on the beach and around the harbour – and long may it continue – but for the younger ones, I was wondering if we might find space to put up a climbing frame and swings like they have in Littlehampton."

He put his sherry down on a nearby table and pulled a scroll from the inner pocket of his jacket. Once unrolled, it was a drawing of a playground.

"A dedicated park?" said Kate.

"Yes, I'd be happy to build it in my spare time at no cost beyond the materials. If there's enough space, we could add more later: a six-seat rocking horse, a sandpit…"

"You see, this is the sort of thing that justifies having this function. I can go over to a councillor and put the idea directly to them. And believe me, I will. Thank you, Mr Patterson. Have a fruitful evening."

Kate's next stop was to be Desmond Ainsley… but Piers Drysdale, the vicar at St Matthew's stepped in front of her.

"Mrs Forbes, how fortunate we should bump into each other."

"Good evening, Reverend Drysdale. Are you backing Sandham?"

"Indeed I am. At least, I'm hoping to with a rather good idea. The fence around the southern boundary of the church is falling apart. I think we can both agree it's not conducive to creating a good impression for the town's visitors."

"That sounds like maintenance, vicar. Perhaps the bishop is the best person to talk to."

"It was the bishop who suggested I talk to you, Mrs Forbes."

Kate assumed that 'suggested' meant 'insisted'.

"Well, of course, this is primarily an ideas forum. For example, along by the river, there's a spot that would be ideal for picnics. The problem is access. I was thinking we could clear the area, create a dedicated path from the lane, and put in some benches and tables. I'm also looking for somewhere to put a visitor information office. Perhaps a small shop by the harbour. It's not cheap though. Perhaps the Church might support it with funds?"

"Ah, funds are short at the moment," said the vicar, possibly wondering how to report back to his boss that he'd been outflanked.

"The Sandham sponge cake!" declared Mr Dexter, the baker who had appeared at Kate's side.

"Pardon?"

"You're looking for ideas. People will flock for miles to come and try a slice of Sandham sponge."

"Oh, it's special, is it?"

"Well, have you ever enjoyed a Victoria sponge?"

"Yes, it's delicious. Is Sandham sponge similar?"

"No, it has a completely different name."

"Er… yes… but the cake itself?"

"Oh, it's a Victoria sponge, but *with a different name*. What do you think?"

"Well, it would certainly provoke a strong reaction…"

But before Kate could seriously discourage the idea of negating Queen Victoria's connection to the noted jam sponge, silence fell on the room. It was the arrival of Miles Longbottom, heir to his father's title and estate. While his tall frame, wavy brown hair and stylish mid-grey blazer was hardly a conversation stopper, the whopping bruise on his left cheek certainly was.

"Just got here from the railway station," he explained to those ogling him. "Bit of a delay with the signals outside London. Anyone seen my father?"

"Lord Longbottom's up the end," said Fred Brigstock, the farmer.

"Right…"

Kate nodded and offered a 'good evening' as he passed.

She knew the situation, of course. Should the Sandham initiative be successful, its future would best be served by a man younger than Herbert. Who better than Herbert's eldest son?

Kate smiled in all directions as she moved off in a circuitous route to make sure she ended up neither too near nor too far from Lord Longbottom by the tables at the other end of the room.

Successfully doing so, she was soon able to hear snatches of their conversation, which for some reason was conducted in low voices. All she could get was a sense of something being wrong in London, to which Lord Longbottom muttered, "It's probably wise to not trouble the police."

At this, Kate could only wonder – was this the serious business his lordship mentioned on Sandham Promenade?

Five

Kate joined Pru Davenport and her husband, Sir Christopher.

"Kate," said Pru, looking graceful in a plum tweed twinset and pearl necklace, "I expect you noticed…"

"I did," said Kate.

"I've no idea what you two have noticed," said Sir Christopher, "but young Longbottom's taken quite a clump."

"My, you look smart, Christopher," said Kate, changing the subject. He did look smart too in a mustard blazer and crimson bow-tie.

"It's a jolly thing you're doing, Kate," he said. "Have you got a list of wallets you want to prise open?"

"Not yet – it's mainly ideas at this stage."

Kate mentioned her picnic idea and drew some unworkable suggestions from the pair.

While listening, she watched Miles Longbottom withdraw from his father's side to talk to others. He was replaced immediately by Desmond Ainsley.

Pru took a sip of sherry and eyed her friend.

"Kate, in the not-too-distant future, you and the professor would look just right at this kind of function."

"All in good time, Pru."

"A man like that needs balance in his life. It shouldn't be all dusty old volumes and muddy archaeological digs. He needs the love of a good woman. Otherwise, there's a danger he'll lose all perspective. I remember a Professor Randall from before the War. Do you remember him, Christopher?"

Kate looked to Sir Christopher, who seemed to have developed a fascination for the ceiling.

"Uh…?"

Pru pushed on. "Yes, John Randall… Honestly, Kate, sixty years of age, of which fifty were spent alone in a library. Conversation? When I met him for the first time, he never said hello. He simply asked to what degree, if any, had Eleanor of Aquitaine's interest in chivalric literature influenced future English rulers. I was well prepared to discuss the weather, but that left me stumped."

Kate smiled but was looking around the hall. Her gaze soon halted at the Chief Constable of Sussex, Sir Ronald Hope, looking relaxed in a well-worn grey suit.

"A word to the wise," said Sir Christopher, "the police never have any money, and they're often short of ideas."

But Kate suddenly spotted a better target. Desmond Ainsley had just finished talking with Lord Longbottom and was lighting a cigar as he headed back her way.

She made her move.

"Mr Ainsley!"

"Mrs Forbes, a pleasure. We haven't spoken in ages."

"What I'm thinking is this, Mr Ainsley. We get a good number of visitors each year, but how many of them return? I propose that we carry out surveys every week across next summer to find out who's a first timer, who's a regular, what they like about Sandham, what disappoints them, and if a Visitor Information Office might be the way forward."

"Are you after money?"

"Money is one of my aims…"

"Doesn't the Crown Hotel put leaflets out at the reception desk?"

"Mr Ainsley, I'm talking about interacting with our visitors in a completely new way."

"Mrs Forbes, didn't I hear a whisper you might seek election to the town council?"

Back in the summer there had been talk of her seeking a seat. She still had a few reservations about that though.

"Possibly not," she said.

"But you must! Your late husband's reputation would easily carry the day for you. Then you could get that lazy lot to pay out of their own funds to promote the town."

"Yes, well…"

Just then, Mrs Jennings, the mayor's wife came alongside.

"Mr Ainsley…"

"Ladies, ladies, no need to fight over me."

Desmond then puffed happily on his cigar while Mrs Jennings made an inane observation about the weather.

Kate needed a way back in. Everyone knew that Mr Ainsley was separated from his wife, although not divorced. He generally passed it off as a matter of her preferring to live with her family in London. Then there was his daughter, Amelia, a vacuous, big spender who turned up occasionally to let people know how fabulous she was. There was talk of her marrying soon into the Faulkner-Smythe family who, according to Pru, were an appallingly snobbish, titled bunch based in Surrey.

Yes, she would ask Desmond Ainsley about his wonderful daughter.

But farmer Fred Brigstock cut her off.

"I hear you're looking for ideas."

Kate beheld him. While she didn't know him personally, she knew he owned farmland just outside Sandham. She had also heard he was selling off parts of it.

"It's Mr Brigstock, isn't it?"

"That's right. I was wondering about my meadow."

"Ah…" This sounded potentially costly.

"I'm wondering about holding a medieval re-enactment. I've seen it elsewhere. People dress up, there's horses and jousting… It'll get the visitors in for a reasonable price."

Kate brightened.

"That's a wonderful idea, Mr Brigstock. Are you sure you can spare the land? Only, I've heard you're selling off parts of your farm."

"Oh, just a small part. No, the meadow's fine for summer events."

"Well, I have a little notebook and I'm going to jot down some of the ideas we get this evening. Yours will be among them. Thank you."

Kate rejoined Pru, only half paying attention while she wrote down Messrs Patterson's and Brigstock's ideas. By the time she had finished, Pru was chatting with headmaster Guy Royston.

"Mr Royston has exciting plans for next summer," she told Kate, by way of a catch-up. "He's to do the grand tour of Europe."

"Oh, it won't be the whole thing," said Guy. "Far from it. My wife and I…" He nodded to Hilda, talking with someone nearby. "We're thinking in terms of France and Italy."

"Guy's coming up for retirement," said Pru, "so he thought he and his wife would take a look at the world around them."

"Good for you, Mr Royston," said Kate. "I'm told there's a lot of the world to see. My niece has certainly travelled a bit, including to the Pyramids, but it's never been my passion."

"Oh, it's hardly a passion, Mrs Forbes. Not like your passion for the town. Now that's something. When Lord Longbottom invited me, I thought how I might best assist. I'm thinking I could extol the virtues of Sandham to our many wealthy parents. Perhaps sailing lessons in the harbour for All Saints boys? I'm sure parents would pay for that sort of thing."

"I'll make a note of it," said Kate, taking out her little book. Certainly, the education provided at All Saints cost a small fortune. Parents sending their sons there would have money.

While she jotted down the suggestion, she thanked Mr Royston and plotted her next target.

That happened to be Mr Deane who, with his wife, ran the Coronation Dining Rooms on East Avenue near the seafront. This encounter, however, was essentially him spending a couple of minutes explaining how civic-funded signposts pointing to his establishment would be good for the town.

Kate thanked him and moved on.

She next tried the mayor, but he was in close conversation with a couple of councillors and her wait on the periphery proved to be in vain for the time being.

Vowing to try again later, she moved on.

But who would she try next?

While looking for another likely target, she overheard a discreet chat between Lord Longbottom and Guy Royston. They seemed to be having words about a painting.

"It's all in hand, Herbert. I've just been busy with new parents, that's all. I'll be very happy to sort it out for you on Monday."

Kate looked elsewhere. Perhaps a word with Miles Longbottom, who was chatting with a boat repair chap. Next to them, Robert Patterson was talking to the owner of the Alhambra. Fred Brigstock and Desmond Ainsley were also in conversation. All Kate caught of it though was Desmond, saying, "Don't worry about it, old friend. Tell him what I told him." But Fred didn't look like a friend at that moment.

Kate meanwhile ended up back with Pru and Sir Christopher, the latter of whom seemed undecided about the quarter sandwich on his plate.

"Any luck?" asked Pru.

"The evening is young," said Kate. "I've jotted down a few ideas, but there's more gold to unearth. That farmer, Fred Brigstock came up with something you'll love. He's suggesting we use his meadow for a medieval re-enactment thingummy with horseback jousting."

"I like the sound of that!" said Sir Christopher. He put his plate down so he could take up imaginary reins and a jousting pole.

"I'll think he'll be able to bear some of the cost too," said Kate. "After all, he's selling some land off. That should boost his coffers."

"Perhaps not as much as you'd think," said Sir Christopher, ceasing his horseback activity to pick his plate up again. "I've heard he's working on a deal with Desmond Ainsley."

"Desmond Ainsley?" queried Kate. "What *isn't* that man involved in?"

Pru's eyes narrowed.

"If fingers in pies were a real measure of a businessman's activities, Desmond Ainsley would need six hands."

Pru had more thoughts on ethical business practice, but Kate was only half listening. From a few feet away, she could partly hear Mrs Deane talking to Lord Longbottom. The nobleman was smiling as he took a gulp of sherry. He then said a few words before a pained expression gripped him. He managed to utter, "Sir Christopher…" – at which point he fell to the floor.

What came next was a scream and lots of confusion… and Miles Longbottom racing to the scene… and a glimpse of Mrs Deane on the floor too… and Desmond Ainsley crying out, "Someone call a doctor!"

Six

Doctor John Howard swept in. He was a serious, balding man in his late fifties and the husband of Kate's friend Ginny. He was followed by the uniformed Sergeant Jones, who the regulars at the Promenade Tea Rooms referred to as Old Grumpy. Trailing these two was Constable Daniel Harris, also in uniform.

Kate and Dr Howard acknowledged each other as he and the sergeant passed her, but Chief Constable Sir Ronald Hope was quick to usher the fresh arrivals to the far end, which had been cleared of everyone apart from Miles Longbottom.

Constable Harris meanwhile stopped in front of the crowd.

"I'm sure some of us would prefer to go home," said someone at the back. This was in response to the Chief Constable's request that everyone should remain.

"They won't be long," said Harris. "It's just a matter of confirming whatever it was. Heart attack, I expect."

Kate had known Daniel Harris, son of Winnie at the Promenade Tea Rooms, his whole life, and recalled saying oochie-coochie to him as a baby. As far as she knew, he'd never had any medical training. That said, a heart attack did seem a reasonable explanation.

In that vein, the next few minutes passed with plenty of speculative muttering before the Chief Constable and Dr Howard returned from the scene. This left Miles Longbottom with his father, and Sergeant Jones, who appeared to be searching around the tables.

"Right…" said the Chief Constable in a way that suggested he had disturbing news. "Dr Howard has confirmed my worst fear. Lord Longbottom died due to poisoning."

There was an audible gasp.

"Most likely cyanide crystals added to something he drank," said the doctor, which sparked more consternation.

"He was drinking sherry just before he collapsed," said the Chief Constable. "I'll have his glass tested for traces of the drug. We'll also check for fingerprints."

"If I might see Mrs Deane…?" the doctor prompted.

"She's recovering in the room next door with her husband and Lady Davenport," said Kate.

"Does that mean we're free to leave?" asked Desmond Ainsley as the doctor left the room.

"No," said the Chief Constable. "We'll be taking statements from everyone in due course, but obviously that's going to take some time. With that in mind, did anyone see anything suspicious?"

"His lordship's last words might help," said Mr Swithin. "He gasped 'Sir Christopher' and then dropped dead."

"I see." The Chief Constable turned to a clearly disconcerted fellow knight. "Does that tally with your own recollection of events?"

"Well…" began Sir Christopher, "I was nearby and I saw him drink his sherry… and then he sort of looked pained… and then he gasped Sir Christopher!"

"Which you'll agree is your name."

"Yes, I'm aware of that, Ronald."

"Do you mind me asking – did you kill Lord Longbottom?"

Sir Christopher's eyebrows shot up.

"Of course not!"

"Um… 'of course not' you don't mind me asking? Or 'of course not', you didn't kill him?"

"The latter! Herbert was an old friend!"

"What were you doing at the time – apart from watching, I mean."

"I was examining a cheese sandwich."

"You thought it was suspicious?"

"No, I was wondering why they put brown pickle in them. I'm more a tomato man. Still, I suppose it's getting late in the season."

"Tomatoes and pickles aside, Sir Christopher, did you see anything suspicious?"

"Not at all. Everyone was behaving impeccably."

"And yet someone poisoned Lord Longbottom."

"Yes... they did."

"You're not fooling anyone, Davenport," said Desmond Ainsley. "Lord Longbottom gave us your name."

Kate erupted. "Nonsense! Sir Christopher wouldn't hurt a fly."

"Greenfly maybe," said Sir Christopher with a shrug.

A horrible thought stuck Kate. The death of Lord Longbottom, as bad as it was, would soon be dragged into the realms of lurid sensationalism when the newspapers got hold of the story. Inevitably, first on the scene would be the two-faced Colin Nelson of the Sussex Chronicle. It occurred to her to spend the next few days hiding at home.

Just then, Mrs Deane came in with Pru Davenport and the doctor to a general outpouring of relief.

"Ah," said Sir Ronald. "It's good to see you on your feet, Mrs Deane. Might you be fit enough to confirm something?"

"Yes, Chief Constable. What is it?"

"I've been told that Lord Longbottom's final words were 'Sir Christopher'. It's cast a degree of suspicion, as you can imagine."

Mrs Deane seemed surprised.

"Lord Longbottom and I were discussing gardening. Hanging baskets, to be precise. It was an idea to hang them outside our dining rooms next summer to impress visitors. His lordship liked the idea and suggested I talk to someone here with a love of gardening. He said, 'The man you need to speak to is… Sir Christopher.' Then he… well… you saw for yourselves."

"That settles that then," said Sir Christopher. "It wasn't me!"

"It would seem so," said Sir Ronald.

"It's the motive you should be looking at," said Desmond Ainsley. "The killer will be someone who gains."

He noticeably looked towards Miles Longbottom.

Meanwhile Sergeant Jones had finished his search and was shaking his head.

"No sign of a poison container," he said. "It could be the killer's still in possession of it."

This had everyone eyeing everyone else, although Fred Brigstock merely harrumphed.

"Unless the killer popped out to the little boys' or girls' room and got rid of it on the way."

This caused yet more consternation.

"Alright, alright…" said Jones in an attempt to calm them.

"I was near the door the whole time," said Mr Norris, a grocer by trade. "Apart from Mr and Mrs Deane and Lady Davenport, no one left the room for at least ten minutes before the death."

"It wasn't me," said Mr Deane. "I was alongside Lady Davenport the whole time."

"The killer still has the poison then," said Mr Swithin. "Oh dear…"

"You're not in danger," said Sir Ronald.

"I'm happy to be searched," suggested Mrs Royston. "To allay fears."

"I don't mind being searched either," said Pru Davenport. "I've nothing to hide."

"Me too," said Sir Christopher.

"You're not searching me," said Desmond Ainsley. "It's out of the question."

"Nor me," said Fred Brigstock.

"Well, I don't mind," said the vicar.

"Neither do I," said Robert Patterson.

"That's very public-spirited of you all," said Sir Ronald to those who began showing empty pockets and handbags containing innocent items — all of which Sergeant Jones waved away.

"What's that!" gasped Mr Swithin. He was standing next to Robert Patterson who had pulled a small flat medicine bottle from his jacket pocket.

"I'm not sure," said Patterson.

"It's not the poison, is it?" gasped Fred Brigstock.

"He's the killer!" cried Desmond Ainsley.

"There's your motive too," said Mr Swithin. "This man had a serious falling out with Lord Longbottom a few years back."

"If you wouldn't mind?"" said Sergeant Jones to Patterson.

Robert Patterson duly handed over the bottle, which Jones opened and tapped on the table to release a few crystals. He then turned to Constable Harris.

"Take him to the station."

Harris nodded and took hold of Patterson's arm.

"I'm innocent," protested Patterson. "I haven't done anything. Please… somebody help."

"Let's go, shall we?"

"Right," said Sir Ronald, "I'll get someone from Scotland Yard to look into this tomorrow."

"Why bother when it's cut and dried?" said Desmond Ainsley – but Sir Ronald ignored him.

As Robert Patterson was escorted out of the room, Kate thought that bringing in Scotland Yard was a sensible step. Justice would always be paramount in her mind. That said, something about this whole business seemed too convenient.

Was Robert Patterson a ruthless killer?

Kate could only wonder what her niece, Lady Jane Scott would make of it.

Seven

Wrapped in a cream cardigan, Kate was sitting by the fire at home, staring at the glow while she sipped warm cocoa. Although it had been a lovely bright day, the evening had turned a little chilly.

It would a difficult night for sleep.

It was still hard to believe that Lord Longbottom was dead from poisoning and that Robert Patterson was in custody pending the arrival of a detective from Scotland Yard.

She tried to see how it could have happened. A calm individual, moving among them, administering cyanide, talking, laughing, arguing a point, looking innocent…

But who would risk the hangman's rope to bring Herbert Longbottom's life to an end?

She thought of the mechanics. No one would sprinkle cyanide crystals into someone else's drink. Too risky. But they might add the crystals to their own drink. Then it would be a straightforward matter of waiting for the opportunity to swap glasses. At the right moment, it could be done in a couple of seconds.

Kate shuddered and picked up the *Woman's Life* magazine Pru had passed on to her. Her friend had mentioned an article about whether women should keep secrets from their husbands. She stared at the page for a moment then put it down again.

Somewhere outside, a fox shrieked.

The case against Robert Patterson seemed to be cut and dried. But why would he show them the bottle of poison willingly? Why not hang on to it in the hope of leaving the town hall without anyone searching him?

She sighed and rose from her chair, wishing for something pleasant to think about.

Professor Peregrine Nash popped into her head – an image of him smiling beneath a straw hat in the sunshine.

Placing her cup on the sideboard, she went to the window and peered outside. All was dark and quiet.

Of course, you couldn't rush things, but she hoped their friendship might continue to develop rather than fizzle out like a faulty firework. The last thing she wanted was for society's expectations to decide her future. And yet, she respected the past and the standards established long ago. It was a tricky balance to get right.

She glanced at her small oil painting of a countryside cottage in summertime with verdant fields beyond stretching away to distant hills. It looked so idyllic and peaceful.

What of Jane? What were her plans? Not just in archaeology, but in life.

Kate returned to her fireside chair.

Jane's father seemed unfazed in his last letter. He cited Jane's fierce independence as something to celebrate rather than see it purely as something that hindered her chances of matrimonial bliss. In other words, he wouldn't be joining those in her wider family who wanted to see her married off quickly to anyone suitable. Kate had written back to him, agreeing wholeheartedly with his views on the subject.

It was ironic then that Kate's glimpse of future happiness for herself had come via Jane's connection to the University of Oxford and one of its professors, Peregrine Nash.

But Jane and marriage? There was more chance of herself and Perry marrying first.

A knock at the door made her jump.

She glanced at the clock on the mantlepiece. It was half-past nine. Who would call at such an hour?

"Hello?" she answered at the closed front door.

"Mrs Forbes?" It was a woman's voice.

"Yes?"

"It's Mrs Patterson. My son, Robert, is in a bit of trouble. I heard you were at the town hall earlier."

A very concerned Kate opened the door to a woman she knew a little, having seen her around the town over the years. Unsurprisingly, the look on Mrs Patterson's face was one of fear.

"Come in. We can talk by the fireside."

A few minutes later, with Mrs Patterson nursing a cup of cocoa, the polite preliminaries were over and the two were left facing the awful situation.

"He's been staying with me while he settles back into Sandham life. When he got that invitation to attend the function, he was overjoyed. But now…"

"Unfortunately, these things happen, Mrs Patterson. Sometimes, men and women take extreme measures if driven to it."

"Could you help?"

The question caught Kate off-guard.

"Help? In what way?"

"They believe my son murdered Lord Longbottom, but he's innocent."

Kate wondered what to say to the mother of a man who might soon have an appointment with the hangman.

"Well, the police are dealing with it… and they do seem to have some incriminating evidence."

"He wouldn't do it. He had no reason."

Kate thought back to the aftermath of the murder.

"Mr Swithin mentioned a history between your son and Lord Longbottom."

"Mr Swithin, the bank manager?"

"Yes, Mr Swithin and his lordship were friends."

Mrs Patterson seemed reluctant to expand on it.

"Yes... well... there's some truth in it. We're an army family. Robert's father, God rest his soul, was a major. His father's father was a captain who served for a time with Lord Arthur Longbottom, Herbert's father. There was a good-natured family hope that Robert would continue the advancement by becoming a colonel."

"Hmm," said Kate, "so, what happened?"

"Just after the Great War, my Robert was one of five young officers messing around on an assault course without permission. One of them fell and broke his neck. Lord Herbert Longbottom was the commanding officer at the time. He called for a Court of Inquiry and these young officers were stripped of their commissions. They all left the army after that. I don't mind telling you my Robert took it very badly."

"So, he blamed Lord Herbert Longbottom for ending his military career?"

"That's what it'll look like when the police find out all the details. But Robert dusted himself down and began a new life. He took work on building sites and trained as a carpenter. When he returned to Sandham, he didn't come to do anyone harm. He's been building himself up as a skilled man. He has a small business now."

"Yes, he told me. A yard and an apprentice – and plenty of work."

"Exactly. He went to that function to make connections with the right people. He didn't go there to kill anyone."

Kate could only shrug.

"I'm not sure what I can do. The Chief Constable himself was there. I'd imagine there will be pressure for an early resolution."

"You have experience, Mrs Forbes. I know all about your escapades with Lady Jane."

"Yes, but… if there are fingerprints on the glass or…"

"I'll pay you."

Kate was shocked.

"Mrs Patterson, I'm not a consulting detective."

"Name your price. I have money."

"No, really, I don't want your money."

Mrs Patterson took a moment to blow her nose on a faded handkerchief.

"They're going to hang my son for murder, Mrs Forbes. I don't know who else to turn to."

"Mrs Patterson…"

"Yes?"

Kate studied that hopeful face with the intent of letting her down gently. Instead, she found herself saying, "Go home and try to rest. I'll have a think about it overnight."

"Thank you, Mrs Forbes. I'm sure between you and your niece, you'll find the truth and save my son."

A few moments later. Kate waved her off at the front door.

Consulting detectives?

It seemed ridiculous.

And yet, and yet…

Kate closed the door and stared at the telephone in the nook under the stairs. The question now was a simple one. Would she make a late evening call to a number in Berkeley Square, London?

Eight

Low morning sunshine streamed through Kate's front windows to warm her in a wingback armchair after a breakfast of soft-boiled eggs, toast and coffee.

Unsurprisingly, her thoughts had been stuck on the business of murder ever since Mrs Patterson came round the previous evening. Kate was meant to be thinking of ways to keep Sandham uppermost in visitors' minds. Having it become the South Coast's murder capital would no doubt achieve it for her, but hardly in the best way.

She thought about last night's call to Jane. It had seemed strange to suggest that they might become unofficial consulting detectives on the basis that Mrs Patterson had offered to pay them. The novelty and seriousness of the situation had sat together awkwardly though, and still did.

Kate rose from her chair and went to the front window where she beheld several sparrows squabbling in a bush off to one side. Then the postman came along and pushed something through her letterbox.

As he continued on his way, she wondered, in practical terms, what she and Jane might offer Mrs Patterson.

She sighed and went to retrieve the post. It was a letter from Perry Nash – she could tell by the handwriting. A moment later, she was reading the contents.

> Dear Kate,
>
> I'm very much looking forward to our lunch date on Saturday. I'll be arriving at Sandham Station at 11:20. It was very kind of you to offer to pick me up from there. Thank you.
>
> Until Saturday.
>
> Fondest regards,
>
> Perry

Kate smiled and read it again. She could hear his voice speaking the words. It also pleased her that his 11:20 arrival would leave plenty of time for a lovely stroll along the promenade before lunch.

She would respond immediately.

What to write?

Perhaps she would avoid any mention of murder.

No, Perry wasn't someone she could hide things from. That was never a good basis for…

For what?

No, Perry had no idea who Lord Longbottom was. News of his demise would keep.

A moment later, she was at the dining room table poised over a blank sheet. Previously, she'd used 'Dear Perry' and signed off with 'Yours Sincerely, Kate'… but Ginny's idea to spice things up came to mind.

"Perhaps some minor modifications…"

> Dearest Perry,
> Thank you for confirming our arrangements. I'm also very much looking forward to lunch on Saturday.
> See you at 11:20 at the station.
> Warmest regards,
> Kate

Five minutes later, she was strolling down Cobb Lane with a lightness of spirit carrying her on a mission to buy a stamp and post the letter.

At the end of the lane, she turned right towards the harbour and the old part of town, where the post office was situated. This was the part of the High Street that visitors enjoyed, with its twists and turns and narrow side streets. She hummed a pleasing tune as she waved to the lady in the florist's, glanced in the window of the souvenir shop, passed the closed amusement arcade and ice cream parlour, nodded to the newsagent, smiled at the women in the ladies' hairdresser and the man in the motor garage.

As she arrived at the post office though, Dorothy Drysdale, the vicar's wife came out.

"Oh! Mrs Forbes. What a shocking business last night."

"Yes, shocking is the word for it, Mrs Drysdale."

"It's not in the papers yet, but it soon will be. Do you know Robert Patterson?"

"Not really, no."

"I saw him the other day. I never had him down as a killer. Still, they say you can never tell. I certainly couldn't, but I've met a few people today who say they knew he was rotten all along."

"Really?"

"What side of the fence are you on, Mrs Forbes? Seeing as you know about these things."

"I'm really no expert."

"You and Lady Jane won't be getting involved then."

"No, not at all. Lady Jane *is* coming down, but not to solve a crime."

"Ahh, she must be such a comfort for you. How long is it since you lost dearest Henry?"

For some reason, Kate suddenly felt the weight of the letter in her hand.

"Sixteen months."

And that was the truth of it. Sixteen short months.

Hardly any time at all.

Dorothy Drysdale smiled sweetly.

"Look after yourself, Mrs Forbes."

Kate nodded and watched her head down towards the quayside.

As if from the sky, guilt landed on Kate's shoulders like a heavy, invisible cloak. She wasn't sure how much time was meant to pass before one could live again, but sixteen months suddenly seemed disrespectfully short. After all, didn't Queen Victoria wear black for half a century?

She put the letter to Perry in her bag and crossed the High Street bound for Church Lane. She would write a fresh version later.

In her mind though, the fresh version began to form all by itself.

> Dear Professor,
> I'll meet you at the station as arranged.
> Lunch will be at the Crown Hotel at one o'clock.
> Yours sincerely,
> Kate Forbes

Nine

It seemed appropriate for it to be the vicar's wife bringing some respectability to proceedings. It was also sobering that Kate's route to Pru's house should take her past St Matthew's Church. Doubtless, that fine 12th century establishment had encountered far more serious matters than her current tribulations.

She paused by the lychgate. Not to enter church grounds, but to reflect. Who else had stood here over the long centuries with a troubled mind?

She looked up to the bell tower, which had been added in the 14th century. Jane loved this place. It was she who would tell anyone who lingered how the monks had built over an earlier Saxon church, and that remnants of the original were still visible in the lower walls of the nave.

From the church, she pushed on, past the old graveyard and the larger modern cemetery, and along the tree-lined lane to where it met Burnt Ash Lane. A right turn here quickly brought her to Fairmile House, home of Sir Christopher and Lady Davenport.

The house itself – early Georgian, painted cream, with a small portico entrance – was set back from the road behind open double gates. Inside were two parked cars: the Davenports' green Alvis tourer, and a burgundy and black Triumph Super Seven four-seater, the latter of these containing her niece.

"Hello, Aunt Kate," said Jane hopping out of the vehicle. "What good timing."

They hugged.

"Jane, I bet you weren't expecting to be back so soon."

"No, but it's important."

"I expect Harry was disappointed."

"Not at all. He understands. Besides, we can meet up any time."

"Yes, of course you can."

Any further thoughts were cut short by Fossett, the Davenports' butler, opening the front door to them.

"Mrs Forbes, Lady Jane, you're expected. Sir Christopher and Lady Davenport are in the sitting room."

"Thank you, Fossett," said Kate as he stood aside to let them in. She had telephoned first thing, putting Pru on the back foot regarding whether the police had detained the right suspect.

They entered the spacious sitting room to find not much sitting going on. Pru and Christopher were pacing up and down like a couple of tormented souls in a gilded cage of large mirrors, oil paintings of birds, elegant lamps and padded red velvet sofas either side of a white stone fireplace – all this enhanced by a fine view of a beautiful rear garden.

"Fossett, coffee for our guests," said Pru, without breaking stride.

"And could you bring a sherry glass, please," said Jane. "An empty one. I'm assuming they're similar to the ones used at the town hall."

"They are," said Pru.

"I'll think we'll sit," said Kate. "Otherwise, the four of us will wear out the rug."

"We're still in a state of agitation," said Sir Christopher.

Pru agreed. "I'm still in shock that someone thought, even for a moment, that my husband could be involved in murder."

Kate had slept on it and hadn't lost the focus she'd had when she called Jane last night.

"Lord Longbottom had a serious matter to deal with, and he'd intended to speak to someone about it at the town hall last night."

"Was one of those Patterson?" asked Jane.

"I don't think Herbert actually talked to Patterson."

"When you called me last night, you said it emerged that Patterson and Lord Longbottom had history from their army days. Would that have been water under the bridge or a continuing grudge?"

"I don't know, Jane."

"The police will believe the latter," said Sir Christopher, "because Patterson had the poison in his pocket. The question is – is it too convenient?"

"He protested his innocence," said Kate. "Although we shouldn't be swayed by that."

"Well," said Jane, "it seems worthy of a closer look. I'd imagine the killer put the poison in their own glass, rather than try to pour cyanide crystals into Lord Longbottom's."

"My thoughts, too," said Kate. "That way, at the opportune moment, it would be a quick swap of two identical glasses. It could be done in an instant."

"And avoiding leaving fingerprints wouldn't be too difficult," added Jane.

"Then it's just a question of who," said Pru.

Sir Christopher clapped his hands together.

"I'm way ahead of you!"

"In what way?" said Pru, but her husband was already leaving the room.

"From what I understand," said Jane, "plenty of people had the opportunity to commit the crime. We need to narrow things down by looking into motives."

"I've thought about this all night," said Kate. "Miles arrived with a bruised cheek, which could be related to the serious business troubling Herbert."

"The motive might be inheritance," said Pru. "It wouldn't be the first case of it."

"To counter that," said Kate, "he would have become the next Lord Longbottom anyway, in due course."

Pru shrugged. "Perhaps he was in a hurry. After all, there's sure to be some money that comes with the title."

Sir Christopher returned, smiling broadly and holding a black chalkboard and easel.

"I had this set up in the other room. Won't take a jiffy…"

Once the board was on the easel, he stood to one side, leaving Kate to wonder what she was seeing.

"It's a murder board," he prompted.

To Kate, it looked like he'd drawn several matchstick men with dotted lines connecting some of them.

Pru smiled apologetically.

"When you telephoned earlier with the possibility of a miscarriage of justice, my dear husband said he'd get cracking."

Kate smiled in complete understanding. Sir Christopher had spent most of his life as a civil servant. Indeed, six years ago, he received his knighthood for services to his country. It was just that Kate always got the feeling that his greatest qualification for the job had been his excellent family connections. For instance, his uncle was a baron. That said, Kate thought Sir Christopher Davenport was one of the loveliest and gentlest men anyone could wish to meet – even if he often came over as a crackpot.

"Right then, our suspects," he said.

"They all look the same," Kate pointed out.

"Surely not? They're different colours."

"Is the middle one Robert Patterson?" asked Jane.

"No, that's the chief constable. He's in blue chalk, you see. Robert Patterson is on the right in red, next to Miles Longbottom in green."

"Who's the other green one?" asked Pru.

"Desmond Ainsley. I've only got three chalks."

"I'm not sure it helps us," said Kate.

"I couldn't fit everyone on the board. I mean, obviously we also have to consider revolutionaries. Or, even worse… Lord Longbottom was President of the Cricket Club, and there was recently some cheating in a match. I never liked the look of that umpire…"

But Jane stepped closer to the board.

"Were there revolutionaries or a cricket umpire at the town hall?"

"Er… no."

"Then we've begun the process of narrowing the field."

Kate was about to agree, but Fossett knocked and entered.

"Coffee won't be long, Sir Christopher, but there's a Chief Inspector Ridley of Scotland Yard at the front door. Should I show him in?"

Ten

Ridley came in – short grey hair, early-to-mid forties, standing tall in a plain, navy-blue suit. He looked a little tired, but also ready to get started, which pleased Kate. She and Jane had assisted him with three cases to date, and he was what most people would consider 'a good copper.'

"Mrs Forbes? Lady Jane?"

"Welcome back to Sandham," said Kate.

"Thanks. It's good to see you again." He turned to the homeowners. "Lady Davenport, Sir Christopher… I see you're all acquainted."

"We've been friends with Kate forever," said Pru. "And as for Jane, since she was a girl."

"Yes, well, it saves me a journey later."

"*Chief* Inspector?" said Kate, querying his rise in rank.

"A recent promotion," said Ridley. He made it sound only marginally more momentous than having a new hat.

"Congratulations," said Jane.

"Well deserved," said Kate.

Ridley looked keen to move on – but had to stifle a yawn.

"An early start, obviously," said Pru.

Ridley shrugged. "A late-night call and a train at the crack of dawn. All in a day's work."

"You must join us for coffee," said Sir Christopher. "It'll perk you up a treat."

"No, thank you. I won't keep you long. You won't be surprised to know I'm here regarding the unfortunate death of Lord Longbottom."

Pru nodded to Fossett, who departed.

"How can we help?" she asked the detective. "We've already given statements."

"Yes, I've read yours and Sir Christopher's statements, and yours too, Mrs Forbes, but you've all had a night's sleep. Sometimes recollections emerge after an interval."

"True," said Sir Christopher. "Do take a seat, old chap."

"Thanks," said Ridley, doing so.

"Um… I hope I'm not a suspect," said Sir Christopher. "If you'd care to look at my board, you'll see it can't be me."

Ridley turned to the chalkboard.

Kate, being nearest Ridley, heard him mutter, "Good grief…"

"My husband has a few theories," said Pru. "You may want a large brandy."

"No, thank you, Lady Davenport."

Kate smiled, but Ridley was keen to press on.

"First things first. Sir Christopher, you're not a suspect. However, I've been told you knew his lordship well. Perhaps you could throw some light on his recent state of mind."

"Not me, Chief Inspector. Prior to the town hall event, neither Pru nor I had seen him in a couple of weeks."

Ridley's gaze shifted to Kate.

"Mrs Forbes…?"

"Yes… well… you'll have read it in my statement, but yesterday on the promenade, Lord Longbottom told me he had a serious matter on his mind, and that he would speak with the relevant individual at the town hall."

"Yes, I read it, but he never identified the individual or what the concern was. To be honest, Mrs Forbes, your statement makes everyone look like a suspect."

"No, but I didn't mention that Herbert had lunch with Francis Swithin, the manager of the Southern Counties Bank."

"Why not?"

"Because Lord Longbottom told me he wasn't involved. Thinking about it now, that doesn't mean Mr Swithin is completely clueless."

"Alright, I'll have a word with him."

"Do you think it's a cut and dried case?" asked Pru.

Ridley responded with a poker face.

"Robert Patterson is the most likely suspect. I just want to make sure we don't make any mistakes."

"Not investigating other suspects right away might be a mistake," said Jane. "If the case against Patterson isn't watertight…"

Ridley gave the tiniest shrug.

"From what I've learned, Patterson had a long-standing grudge against his lordship. And there's the small matter of him being caught with the poison."

"Hardly caught," said Kate. "He was as surprised as anyone to find it in his pocket."

"Possibly a ruse, Mrs Forbes."

"How?" asked Pru.

"A cornered criminal might try to make it look like someone's set them up."

"I'd imagine the Chief Constable of Sussex expects a speedy resolution," said Jane.

"He does," said Ridley. "I'll take a proper look though."

"Good," said Kate.

"I know Lord Longbottom was a personal friend, but be aware that Sir Ronald Hope has no time for amateurs poking their noses in."

"I see," said Kate. "You mean keep out of it."

Ridley had the opportunity to nod his head or say something to confirm it. He did neither.

"Mrs Forbes, Lady Jane… any small irritation I've felt at your involvement in previous cases is overshadowed completely by my admiration for the way you've managed to find a way to the truth. I'm not a stubborn man. Just like you, I'm driven by one thing only."

"The pursuit of justice?" suggested Kate.

"Exactly so."

"Are you suggesting we *should* get involved then?"

"In a strictly unofficial capacity, yes. By that, I mean if the Chief Constable asks me, I know nothing about it."

Jane's demeanour suggested she was open to the idea. Pru's face meanwhile bore a quizzical expression.

"Are Kate and Jane forming a new police branch?"

"Scotland-Yard-on-Sea?" said Jane with a cheeky grin.

"Absolutely not!" insisted Ridley. His stern expression softened though, even moving somewhat towards a hint of a smile. "Perish the thought!"

"Where's Patterson right now?" asked Jane.

"At Sandham police station. He's denying everything but I'm letting him stew while we wait to see if we get lucky with fingerprints on the glass."

"Might we speak with him?" asked Kate.

"That wouldn't be appropriate. Just do what you usually do. Make a nuisance of yourselves and find out all the gossip. If you're certain something's suspicious, let me know."

"Will do."

Jane was nodding. "I'd say unearthing Lord Longbottom's serious matter might be a priority."

"Absolutely," said Ridley. "Just be aware that it might relate to Patterson. Please don't rule him out as a suspect."

Ridley rose to leave just as Fossett arrived with a coffee pot, four cups, and a sherry glass on a tray, which he placed on the coffee table.

"I'll take that, Fossett," said Jane, lifting the glass by its thin stem.

"It's empty," said Ridley.

"Would you be able to get my fingerprints from it?"

Ridley gave a wry smile.

"No, because you've picked it up in a perfectly correct manner. Fingers on the stem. Also, if you hadn't drawn my attention to it, I wouldn't have noticed that your fingers are in a slightly advanced position meaning your fingertips haven't made contact with the glass, which I have to say is very thin at that point anyway."

"Correct," said Jane. "I doubt you'll get the prints you need."

"No," sighed Ridley.

"Show the Chief Inspector out, Fossett," said Pru. "Happy hunting."

The man from Scotland Yard bade them farewell and followed Fossett out.

"Well, blow me down," said Sir Christopher with a grin. "We're among detectives, Pru."

"Unofficial detectives," said Jane.

"Yes, and not a word to the Chief Constable," said Kate.

Jane smiled at her aunt.

"Uncle would be proud of you."

Kate felt the warmth of the sentiment. Of course, she'd been used to events involving the police long before she and Jane had inadvertently come to solve a few cases. Henry had been a judge who often recounted courtroom tales across the dinner table. Helping Scotland Yard to uncover the truth relating to Lord Longbottom's murder would be a challenge – but one she was sure they could rise to.

"So… suspects?" said Pru.

"There's no shortage of them," said Sir Christopher, indicating the board, "unlike the variety of chalks."

"The shortage is in the realistic alternatives we have," said Kate. "A bottle of poison in one man's possession would persuade many a jury."

"Aunt Kate," said Jane, "could I suggest we start with the other piece of physical evidence we have."

All three looked to her with varying degrees of confusion.

"Other piece of physical evidence?" queried Kate.

"Yes," said Jane. "The bruise on Miles Longbottom's face."

Eleven

Following Kate's directions, Jane was soon steering the Triumph into Hall Lane, which led up to Longbottom Hall.

"Can you remember your first time here, Aunt?"

"Oh, it was a long time ago. Soon after Henry and I were married, I'd say. It was a lunch party. They weren't so keen on dinner parties here. Lunch was their thing. Two dozen guests and a cold buffet."

"Fair enough."

"I think Herbert took after his father. They both preferred to have guests spread about the place, inside and out. I think they felt trapped at a table."

"Did any of their close friends or family ever fall out in a bad way?"

"Not that I know of. It was always very convivial."

Kate spotted the house up ahead on the left – a large, grey stone, two-storey, early Georgian pile with six windows on each side of a four-pillar portico entrance. As far as she knew, the Longbottoms took possession in the 1870s or thereabouts.

"Herbert was an army man then," prompted Jane.

"Yes, until seven or eight years ago. He sort of retired early and became a regular on the social scene hereabouts. That said, he was a champion for Sandham."

Jane brought the car to a halt just short of the gates.

"And what about Miles? Does he have an interest in local matters?"

"Not really. Have you ever met him?"

"Yes, once, at a party in Brighton when I was nineteen or twenty. I remember him smiling at me quite a bit."

"Right, well… these days he's married, has two young sons, and lives in London."

"But he came to Sandham for the function at the town hall."

"Yes, Herbert was keen for him to be there."

"From what I understand, it was being held to test the waters."

"Yes, to see if there was enough commitment to take us forward. I think there was a good level of interest and, despite what's happened, a committee will be formed at some point."

"With Miles heading it?"

"That's the hope. Whether he'll be drawn away from London for tea and biscuits four times a year at the town hall though… who can say?"

Jane pulled away again and drove through the open gates onto a short drive. A moment later, they came to a halt by a freestanding garage – the doors of which were open, revealing the front end of a Rolls-Royce Silver Ghost. Kate supposed Miles would now be the one to drive it.

As they got out of the Triumph, Kate glanced up at the house. A young man was looking down from an upper window. However, it was the craggy-faced butler, Craven who opened the front door to them.

"We telephoned ahead," said Kate.

"Yes, Mrs Forbes. Miss Helen said to expect yourself and Lady Jane, and to show you to the sitting room."

They followed the faithful Craven through a vestibule that, as far as Kate knew, hadn't changed much in all the years the Longbottoms had been responsible for it. While electricity was being rolled out across the region, it had yet to arrive at the hall. Apart from the new telephone line, the household was still very much driven by coal, wood and oil.

"The sitting room," announced Craven, a short way into a corridor off the vestibule. He opened the door and stood aside to let them in.

The room itself was impressive, with a gilt chandelier, three oil paintings of bucolic countryside scenes in the style of John Constable, a large stone fireplace, a faded red three-seater settee facing two wing-back armchairs: one mustard, the other charcoal grey. Between these, on a small plain rug, sat a large oak coffee table with an old, thin, buff-coloured journal or notebook on one end of it.

Over by a tall window overlooking the rear garden, Herbert's daughter, Helen was smiling sadly at them. Kate noticed how her eyes were puffy from a lack of sleep and an abundance of tears.

"Mrs Forbes, Lady Jane…"

"You poor thing, Helen," said Kate, feeling an urge to go over and give her a big hug. She refrained though. "We're both so sorry for your loss."

"Thanks… and please, do take a seat."

Kate and Jane did so. Initially together, but Jane switched at the last second to take a seat opposite her aunt.

"Would you like some tea or coffee?" offered Helen.

"No, thank you," said Kate. "We won't stay long. The thing is, we're absolutely determined that your father receives the justice he deserves."

"Oh, he'll get that, Mrs Forbes. The police have their man."

"Yes… they have. We just want to make sure they're not left with a weakened case because things were rushed through."

"Yes, I see. I don't quite understand how you fit into it though."

"Well, Jane and I don't exactly fit into it. We're more a separate thing on the side."

Helen looked puzzled but Jane smiled.

"It's a good place to be," she said. "We might see things from a different angle or pick up extra information that could assist the police."

"Yes, I've heard all about your exploits," said Helen. "It's just that Miles says this is a watertight case."

"It is," said Miles, entering the room, the bruise on his left cheek still prominent. "Hello, Mrs Forbes… and it's a pleasure to meet you again, Lady Jane. As you can imagine, this is a difficult time for the family."

"You have our sympathies," said Jane.

"We won't take up much of your time," said Kate. "Your father was a dear friend. I just wanted to pay my respects, as did Jane."

"It's much appreciated," said Miles. Perhaps Kate was staring at his face too long, because he added, "You're possibly wondering about my bruise."

"Bruise?" said Kate, innocently.

"I had the misfortune to walk into an open cupboard door."

"Oh, bad luck," said Kate. "I once broke a toe on the leg of a piano. I was barefoot."

"Oww!" said Helen.

"I knew it was there," said Kate, "but I was distracted and, as you say, oww."

Helen nodded, perhaps wondering where all this was going.

"Miles, I must ask," said Kate, "did you know your father had a serious problem on his mind?"

Miles considered it for a second or two.

"He never said anything to me. What about you, Helen?"

Helen shook her head. "No, sorry, Mrs Forbes. I wasn't aware of a problem."

"And Ian wouldn't know," added Miles. "He came back from London with me yesterday. It's his first visit in two years."

"I see…" Kate had hoped Miles might mention his father's advice regarding not troubling the police. "When I spoke with Herbert yesterday lunchtime, he told me something that I believe to be at the heart of the matter. He said he had a serious problem and planned to speak with the appropriate person at the town hall."

Miles shrugged. "Then you just need a list of all those he spoke with."

"We're working on it," said Kate.

"Well, you obviously have a lot to sort out," said Jane as if to bring their visit to an end.

Kate was surprised. This was a tad too soon.

"Oh, I see you've already made a start," added Jane. She was peering at the old document on the coffee table.

Kate leaned forward to read the handwritten title, but the book was facing the other way and could only be read from Jane's seat on the opposite side of the table.

"Father got that out the other day," said Helen. "It's strange though. It hasn't been out of the cabinet in years."

Kate's brow furrowed. "What is it?"

Jane was first to answer. "The Longbottom inventory, Aunt."

Kate's frown remained. She was none the wiser, although she now realised she'd been sleepwalking while Jane had switched seats at the last moment purely to read the title.

"It dates back to when our family first moved here," said Helen.

She came over and picked it up.

"Our grandfather was a collector," she said as she studied the first page. "There must be quite a few hundred items listed… furniture, paintings, ornaments…" She broke into a smile. "The statuette of Venus! We definitely won't find that in the house. Miles broke it."

"I was nine at the time," said Miles, defensively.

But Helen was clearly enjoying this sudden respite.

"He buried it in the garden. Had Father found out, Miles would have lost his allowance for a month."

Miles smiled ruefully before his demeanour changed.

"Hopefully, things will settle down again soon, but first we have a funeral to arrange. And as for the business of murder, we're just glad that the police are on top of things."

He took the inventory from Helen.

"Let's pop this back where it belongs, shall we?"

"Regarding the police," said Kate. "My concern is that their current haste might mean them missing vital evidence."

"I'm sure there's nothing to worry about," said Miles, whose body language was now clearly inviting them to leave. "Any further questions you have regarding our family, ask me directly and I'll give it due consideration."

"Thank you," said Kate taking the hint and rising from her seat.

Jane rose too.

"We're sorry to have troubled you at such a difficult time," she said.

Twelve

A few moments later, they were back outside and heading for the car, with Kate having much to think about. Before she could share any of those thoughts with her niece though, Helen Longbottom came out to catch up with them. She was holding a book with a plain cover.

"Helen?" enquired Kate. "Is everything alright?"

"You'll come to Father's service?" asked Helen. "We're thinking of Monday lunchtime."

"Yes, of course," said Kate.

"We'll both be there," said Jane.

"I'm sorry I didn't mention it earlier."

Kate frowned.

"Are you sure everything's alright?"

"Yes. It's just that… I hate to go against the police, and Miles is certain they have the right man…"

"Helen, what is it?"

"You said Father had a concern. You were right. I went to stay with a friend in Croydon on Friday morning. When I left, Father was in very good spirits."

"And when you returned?" prompted Kate.

"I got back on Sunday morning before church. He was in a very concerned mood by then. I just wish I'd pressed him about it."

"Herbert wouldn't have told you, or me, or anyone else," said Kate. "Don't feel bad about it."

Helen looked ashen. While some had experience of dealing with such matters, others did not.

Kate smiled warmly.

"Helen, you are in our hearts and our thoughts. You and your brothers. My fondness for your father and respect for his memory will be uppermost in anything Jane and I do in connection with this terrible business."

"I know, and I appreciate it. We all do."

"Now you concentrate on your father's commemoration plans."

"I will. Actually, we were thinking of asking Sir Christopher Davenport to give a eulogy at the service. You know him well. Do you think he'd mind?"

Kate beamed. "Sir Christopher and your father were close friends. He'd be honoured."

Helen smiled too. "We'll ask him then."

"I'm sure Sir Christopher will have plenty of stories to tell," said Jane.

Helen smiled again.

"Yes indeed," said Kate. "Plenty of stories to celebrate the life of a fine man."

"Thanks, Mrs Forbes. The town will certainly be a lot less busy without him in action."

Kate laughed softly. "Oh, busy, busy… that was Herbert Longbottom."

Helen fought back a tear.

"I was looking at his appointment diary." She proffered the book she'd been holding. "I don't know if any of it helps."

Kate studied the recent entries then passed it to Jane, who did likewise.

"It's possible there's a clue here," surmised the latter. "He saw Simon Townsend on Friday afternoon… Fred Brigstock and Desmond Ainsley on Saturday… Church on Sunday… then Mr Hilton… Mr Williams… then lunch with Mr Swithin yesterday and the town hall event last night." Jane thought for a moment then continued reading. "Today was meant to be lunch with the Mayor of Sandham. Tomorrow, lunch with the Mayor of Brighton, and a town celebration there in the evening with a hotel room booked. Then Saturday evening back to Sandham for drinks with the Renfrews. Sunday, church, then All Saints School on Monday at nine… drinks at the Crown Hotel at five…" She flicked back. "As you say, he was a very busy man."

Jane mulled it over for a moment longer, then handed the book back to Helen.

"You hang on to it. The police might ask to see it."

"Yes, of course."

"Robert Patterson may well be the right man," said Kate. "We just want to make sure. We owe that much to your father's memory and to Robert's mother, who is worried out of her wits."

"You're looking at it from all sides," said Helen, perhaps coming to appreciate how an investigation worked best. "I wish you well."

They waited for her to go before Jane spoke.

"Miles wouldn't be in his father's appointment diary."

Kate considered it. "No – especially if it were a telephone call."

"It might be worth us having a word with Mr Townsend," said Jane. "He was the first person Lord Longbottom saw after Helen left for Croydon."

"Yes, alright," said Kate. "He wasn't at the function, so he can't be our killer... but..."

"But?"

"It completely slipped my mind, but Robert Patterson is a carpenter who's currently working for Mr Townsend as a subcontractor."

"Oh... that's interesting. Do we know where?"

"Yes, Holton."

"Across the harbour? What are they doing over there?"

"Building houses. I reckon we could catch Mr Townsend at home after work, where it's not a muddy quagmire."

"Aunt, I think we should go to see where Robert Patterson works. You never know what we might learn."

Kate sighed.

"You're right as usual, Jane. Duty first… avoiding mud, second."

Thirteen

Holton was a tiny settlement situated on the western side of Sandham Harbour. The most idyllic way to reach it was to find someone in the vicinity of Sandham quayside willing to offer a leisurely boat trip. Kate and Jane preferred to get answers to their questions quickly though, so drove there.

It wasn't their first visit to Holton. Four months earlier, a certain conspiracy dragged them that way to speak with residents. This time, their journey took them to a plot of land beyond the existing homes, which meant leaving the car at the end of a rutted track. This would no doubt become a lane to the four houses under construction, but at that moment it didn't suit Jane, who feared her Triumph Super Seven might suffer damage to its undercarriage.

"Is there a civic plan for Holton?" she asked as they walked the rest of the way.

"I don't think so," said Kate. "I suppose more homes might eventually mean having a village store and a pub… possibly even a small school, but I haven't heard anything."

Reaching the building site, they beheld a couple of bricklayers at work on the upper floor of the farthest house.

"It's a good day to be outside," said Jane.

"Robert Patterson said when it's sunny but not too hot, he had the best job in the world. He also said that Holton is so peaceful."

"It is."

"He said that sometimes he'd stop work to look out over the fields and the water. Do you know, Jane, I bet he wishes he'd never been invited to the town hall."

Just then, a boy of around fifteen came out to greet them.

"Morning, ladies," he said with a surprising degree of confidence.

"You seem a likely young man," said Kate.

"Jez Wilkes, carpenter, ma'am. Any work you need doing, just let me know. You'll find my prices very reasonable."

"Will I, indeed. How enterprising. However, I don't have any carpentry jobs at the moment."

"No? We had those high winds the other week. No fences down? I'm a dab hand at fence posts."

"No, all fine, thank you."

"Are you Mr Patterson's apprentice?" asked Jane.

"That's right."

Kate's heart sank. The poor young chap was no doubt worried for his future now that his carpentry master had been taken in by the police. She would definitely find some work for him, even if she had to knock down one of her fence posts to provide it.

"I might have some work for you at some point, young man, but for now, we'd like to speak with Mr Townsend."

"This way, ma'am. The mud's quite hard. Last week, you'd have had it up to your—"

"Hello!" called a man in his thirties – possibly just in the nick of time.

"Mr Townsend?" asked Kate.

"Yes, how can I help?"

"I was at the town hall last night."

"Ah…" His smile fell away. "Jez, go and help Tommy."

"Righto, Guv!"

They watched the boy run off round the back of the site.

"Nasty business," said Simon.

"It was," said Kate. "My friend, Lord Longbottom, was poisoned."

"Yes, well… I hear the police have their man."

"Yes, their man being Robert Patterson, who works for you."

Townsend pulled a frown.

"Please don't take this the wrong way, but why are you asking questions about it?"

"We've promised his mother we'd make sure nothing's been overlooked," said Kate. "Were you invited to last night's function at the town hall?"

"Yes, I was invited, but it's not my kind of thing."

"Too stuffy?" asked Kate.

"Something like that."

"What's Robert Patterson like?" asked Jane. "By that, I mean his usual demeanour."

"He always seems calm enough, but I suppose we never know what's in someone's mind, do we."

"Will it affect your work?" asked Kate.

"Losing him? I'll manage. I mean, don't get me wrong, I feel sorry for him. At the end of the day though, I have to look after my own interests."

"Did you have any dealings with Lord Longbottom?"

Simon Townsend flushed slightly.

"No, I barely knew him."

Kate raised an eyebrow.

"We know that's not true, Mr Townsend. We know his lordship had a serious matter playing on his mind and we know he came to see you."

Townsend let out a short huff.

"Alright, he did come to see me about something. It had nothing to do with his death though."

"How can you be sure?"

"What we discussed wasn't worth anyone dying for."

"Can you tell us what it was about then?"

Simon Townsend seemed to weigh it up for a moment before shrugging.

"Alright, I was meant to be working on a housebuilding job at Ridgeway. It's a plot on Fred Brigstock's land. One minute, I'm in for a dozen houses; the next I'm out. His lordship was concerned that something underhand might've taken place. He didn't like that sort of thing spoiling Sandham's reputation."

"Is that job still going ahead?" asked Jane.

"Yes, with someone else at the helm."

"Can you tell us who?"

"A bloke called Desmond Ainsley. He's not a builder; more a money man."

"I see," said Kate, recalling Messrs Ainsley and Brigstock together at the town hall.

"I expect he'll employ the preferred kind of builder before long," said Simon.

"The preferred kind?"

"Someone who's cheap."

"Ah."

"That's the real reason I wasn't at the town hall. I wanted to go because I do believe in the town's future, but… not with him there."

"You and Mr Ainsley are at loggerheads then?"

"Who *isn't* at loggerheads with him? That said, I'm just as annoyed with that blasted farmer. He changed his mind after I'd done unpaid work on estimates, water, drainage reports, and what-have-you."

"He cancelled the work out of the blue?"

"Yes – there's me, about to talk with an architect in Brighton regarding drawings, and Brigstock suddenly says it's off."

"With no explanation?"

"No, none whatsoever. Then, a few weeks later, he changes his mind to do a deal with Ainsley."

"Very annoying," said Kate. "Has this cost you a lot of money, Mr Townsend?"

"Not enough to kill for. The fact is, I've moved on, as you can see."

Kate could indeed see. Simon Townsend was building four semi-detached houses in a less favourable locale. Meanwhile, Desmond Ainsley would soon commence work on a dozen homes much nearer to the railway station and local shops.

"Did Lord Longbottom say anything specific about Mr Ainsley taking over?" asked Jane.

"Not specific, no. He just said he was in favour of my scheme and would have a word with certain people. He's gone now though so that's an end to it. If Desmond Ainsley stitched me up, there's not much I can do about it."

"I suppose not," said Kate.

She and Jane wished him well and returned to the Triumph.

"Desmond Ainsley?" suggested Jane as she started the engine.

"Lunch first, Jane. Then we'll tackle the delightful Mr Ainsley. I have a feeling his version of events might differ from Mr Townsend's."

Fourteen

The sunny October weather was good enough for Kate and Jane to park the car outside Kate's house and stroll down to the sea front. This involved brief conversations along the way with three separate townsfolk regarding events at the town hall and relief expressed by these parties that the police had captured the perpetrator.

Kate and Jane decided it was best not to challenge that view.

Reaching the end of Royal Avenue where it met the promenade, Kate beheld two of her favourite establishments. On the right-hand corner, the Crown Hotel. On the left, their destination – the Promenade Tea Rooms.

On entering, they found just two customers present: retired Colonel Cecil Pickering sitting by the window with a magazine, and Ernie Melton, who was in the corner nursing a cup of tea.

"Lady Jane!" exclaimed Winnie Harris, the owner, from behind the counter. "How are you? We haven't seen you in ages!"

To Kate, this was an all-too-regular reaction to Jane's return, whether she had been away for months or days. On this occasion, it was a single day, although perhaps Jane waving to Winnie from across the street the day before didn't count as a visit.

"I'm well, thanks, Mrs Harris," said Jane with a warm smile. "How are you?"

"Not too bad, thanks, considering the shocking news."

"Mr Melton gave us a full account," said Colonel Pickering.

I bet he did!

"You had a good view from the front steps, did you, Mr Melton?" asked Kate as innocently as possible.

"I spoke with Winnie's boy and the doctor. I'm in full agreement with the police. They have Patterson. He's the one."

Kate found it taxing to smile at a man whose miserable persona somehow spoiled the sunrise yellow décor behind him.

"Are you getting involved then?" asked Winnie.

"Not at all," said Kate. She had no intention of letting them know that she and Jane were unofficial investigators.

"Oh, that's a shame."

"No, it's not," said Ernie. "The town doesn't need people poking their noses in where they're not wanted." He looked to Kate. "No offence."

Kate looked to Winnie.

"We'll have our sandwiches outside. Cheese and pickle for me. Jane?"

"The same please."

"And two teas," added Kate.

Back outside, they took seats by the beach where, for anyone squinting due south against the sun, several boats were visible on a calm sea. Kate looked eastward though, to the rugged coastal path that rose from the end of the flat, orderly promenade to the top of the cliffs fifty feet above the water. It was so good for walkers up there.

She then looked westward to where the promenade ended at a rise to a rocky promontory, the lighthouse, and a spectacular view across the harbour. Again, it was good for walkers who enjoyed getting healthily out of puff.

"I expect you'd prefer to get back to the business of improving Sandham for visitors," said Jane.

"I would. Very much so. I resent having a small-minded murderer throw a spanner in our works."

Just then, Winnie came out with two cups of tea on a tray.

"Did you drive all the way from London?" she asked Jane as she placed their hot drinks on the table.

"Yes, I did this time. It was a good run."

"How's that chap of yours? Harry, isn't it?"

"He's fine, Mrs Harris. He's busy with some research in London."

"It's either old documents or mud, isn't it."

"Yes, that describes history and archaeology perfectly!"

"Oh well, Lady Jane, you never know."

"Thank you, Winnie," said Kate, bringing the encounter to an end.

"Sandwiches in a couple of minutes."

"Righto."

It was a constant rearguard action these days to halt the duty of Winnie and others to ponder Jane's ideal match.

But now something else gate-crashed Kate's thoughts – two people coming along the Promenade from the lighthouse end.

"Jane, don't look, but Guy Royston, the Headmaster at All Saints School, is coming along with his wife, Hilda. They were at the function last night."

Jane glanced nonchalantly in their direction.

"Did they have any connection to Lord Longbottom?"

"Yes, Herbert's sons attended the school."

"Possibly not a way forward then."

"Hello, Mr Royston, Mrs Royston," called Kate. "Do you know my niece, Lady Jane Scott?"

The two came over to stand at the table.

"Hello, Mrs Forbes," said Guy. "Lady Jane, while we've not met, your reputation precedes you. I hear your father is the Earl of Oxley."

"Yes, that's right. Pleased to meet you both," said Jane. "I expect some time away from everything must be just the thing right now."

"Oh yes," said Guy. "It's incredibly busy at the school, but I felt we should take a day away from it all."

"We're still in shock," said Mrs Royston, "as must you be, Mrs Forbes."

"Yes, it was a terrible business… but I'll be alright."

"I've heard good things about All Saints," said Jane. "It has a fine name."

"Oh, thank you, Lady Jane," said Guy Royston. "I'm pleased to hear it."

"My husband has done wonders there," added Mrs Royston.

"Oh nonsense, Hilda. I'm only doing my job. It's actually the school's fortieth anniversary soon, so it's been quite a busy time setting things up."

"Very busy," said Mrs Royston. "Should you ever have sons, Lady Jane, think about All Saints. It's of the right calibre for the grandsons of an earl. It was founded by Sir Owen Rushton's widow, Margaret, whose father was Lord Shepton. Then there was its first trustee, Lord Arthur Longbottom…"

"Hilda…" said Guy, gently chiding his wife.

Kate smiled. This was no doubt a well-used sales pitch.

"Jane and I were wondering why someone would wish harm to Lord Herbert Longbottom. I don't suppose you know anything that might help us?"

"The police have their man," said Guy. "I expect he'll tell them everything in due course."

"Perhaps you could assist us in a little speculation," said Jane. "Why not take a seat for a minute?"

The Roystons smiled uncertainly but did so.

"Are you investigating?" asked Mrs Royston. The idea seemed to excite her.

"No, we're not investigating," said Kate. "As you say, the police have the killer. It's just that, very occasionally, a wrong arrest is made. It's incredibly rare and probably doesn't apply in this case, but there's no harm in having a broader and deeper understanding of events. For example, Lord Longbottom had a serious matter on his mind. Any idea what it might have been?"

Guy shrugged. "No, sorry. Do you think it was related to the school?"

Kate sighed. "Probably not. We believe his mood darkened on Friday or Saturday."

"Well, we never spoke with him. We were staying with Hilda's sister in Eastbourne from Thursday till Sunday afternoon."

"A telephone call perhaps?"

"She doesn't have a phone. But no, before last night, I hadn't spoken with his lordship in ages."

"Last night though – did you discuss anything unusual?"

"No, it was just a brief but passionate chat about the theatre."

"Oh," said Kate. "I thought I heard you discussing paintings."

Guy thought for a moment.

"You're right. We discussed the theatre the previous time we spoke. Yes, paintings. That was it."

"Nothing serious then," said Jane.

"No, not at all."

"Right, well…" said Kate. "Don't let us keep you."

"Have a pleasant afternoon then," said Guy Royston.

Once the Roystons had departed, Kate corrected herself.

"His chat with Herbert. It wasn't about paintings. It was about *a* painting."

"Ha!" exclaimed a voice, making Kate jump. She turned to discover Ernie Melton inside the tearooms but by the open window, meaning he'd been spying on them.

"Mr Melton, privacy should be respected." She felt like adding, 'even by you' but chose not to.

"It's a free country," said Ernie. "At least it was last time I checked."

Winnie came out with their sandwiches.

"Two cheese and pickle."

"Thanks, Winnie," said Jane.

"Was that Mr and Mrs Royston?"

"Yes, it was," said Kate.

"They say he's a hero, putting that fire out. It almost burned the school down."

"Really?" said Jane.

"Rubbish!" said Ernie, still at the window. "The Press made a meal of it."

"I'm sure they didn't," said Winnie.

Ernie huffed. "According to the Sussex Chronicle, it was bigger than the Great Fire of London, when the truth is it was put out by Royston, two boys, and three buckets."

Kate shrugged. "Sensationalism in the newspapers seems to be a curse of our times."

Just then, the roar of a Norton CS1 motorcycle coming down Royal Avenue grabbed their attention. A moment later it stopped by the door to the tea rooms and a young man got off. He failed to notice Kate and Jane sloping off along the promenade, sandwiches in hand.

Thanks to a previous encounter, they knew Colin Nelson as an unscrupulous reporter from none other than the Sussex Chronicle. Not wishing to be reacquainted with the slippery scribe, they made for a distant bench to enjoy their lunch in peace.

Fifteen

Kate and Jane were in the Triumph outside Kate's house. Despite having telephoned ahead, they had yet to set off for the home of Desmond Ainsley because Kate had remembered the fruit pastilles in her cavernous handbag.

"Any red ones left?" asked Jane.

"Last one. Go on."

Jane took the red one from a small white paper bag. Kate took a yellow.

As they sucked their sweets, Kate listened to the birdsong in the trees on an otherwise quiet street. Sometimes, life's ordinary moments were precious.

"It's such a lovely day," said Jane.

"Mmm, the sort of day to be out enjoying ourselves with simple pursuits."

"Yes, a stroll up to the lighthouse, or around the church grounds looking for evidence of history."

"Mmm."

"Instead of which… what do we know about Mr Ainsley?"

"He's involved in everything," said Kate. "By that, I mean everything where there's money to be made. That's not a crime, of course. There are millions of honourable people making money all over the world; it's just that I suspect Desmond Ainsley isn't one of them."

"Has he any convictions for wrongdoing, Aunt?"

"No, and you should ignore me. A few weeks before Henry passed away, Ainsley was rude to him. I've never forgiven him, but we're looking for a poisoner and I mustn't let wishful thinking get in the way."

Jane started the car and they pulled away.

"They say poisoning is the coward's method," she said. "He may yet be our killer. The question is why commit murder rather than, say, throw a punch?"

Kate thought for a moment.

"Ainsley's wealthy and he's separated from his wife. He charges extortionate interest rates to desperate people and buys art, furniture, and cars. If that wasn't enough, his loud, flashy daughter's due to marry into the inexcusably snooty Faulkner-Smythe family. He'll enjoy being able to move in that world. He also hates the idea of joining the town council, because he prefers to be in control of anything he's involved in. And, of course, he's about to start building houses on land owned by Fred Brigstock. It's hard to believe he only came to Sandham two years ago."

"Yes, well, there might be something in this Ridgeway business."

"For Robert Patterson's sake, let's hope so."

Kate gave some brief, simple travel directions, which Jane acknowledged. They would be there in under ten minutes.

Kate enjoyed being driven by her niece. The problem was sleepiness. It would have been marvellous to doze off in the car, but she supposed, as a confidante of a Scotland Yard chief inspector, she ought to remain alert.

She opted for an old trick. Close one eye at a time. Left eye first. Count to ten. Open left eye, close right eye, count to ten. A few turns would…

"Aunt Kate!"

"Eh?"

"I think you might have fallen asleep."

"No, no, I was concentrating on some of the finer points of the case."

"Oh right, only it sounded like snoring."

"No, it's far more likely to be the engine. Probably not firing properly."

It wasn't long before they reached the northeast edge of Sandham where Desmond Ainsley lived on a lush green lane.

"It's just up here on the left," said Kate. "It belonged to an elderly lady called Miss Moore, but she moved in with her sister in Lewes when her health began to fail."

"The red brick one?" asked Jane.

"That's the one. It's called The Brambles. Oh…"

They came to a halt with Kate eyeing a new signpost by the open drive gates. It stated: 'Ainsley House'.

"It's lovely," said Jane, admiring a large, detached, two-storey red brick structure with downstairs white bay windows either side of an arched doorway.

They climbed out of the Triumph, and made their way along the short drive, where a Rolls-Royce Phantom sat off to their left.

Following a knock at the door, they were met with a quizzical look from a chap who Kate presumed to be Ainsley's valet.

"Good afternoon. It's Mrs Forbes and Lady Jane Scott. We phoned ahead. May we speak with Mr Ainsley?"

The valet bowed slightly.

"I'll see if Mr Ainsley is available."

They were kept standing on the doorstep.

"Good job it's not raining," said Kate. "I expect he's worried we might steal the silver."

The valet returned.

"Mr Ainsley will see you in his study. This way, please."

They followed him into a spacious, expensively decorated hallway that boasted a new tiled floor in a black and white herringbone pattern, a regal blue rug, deep crimson floral wallpaper, and a large oil painting of Desmond Ainsley.

The valet knocked on a door at the end of the hallway and pushed it open. He then stood aside to let them into a large pale green room with a white stone fireplace, a variety of oil paintings, a mint green rug on the polished oak floor, and windows that overlooked the garden.

Dressed in another fine suit, Desmond Ainsley rose from a leather chair behind a Georgian oak desk to greet them.

"Mrs Forbes, Lady Jane... welcome to my humble abode. Please do take a seat."

"Thank you," said Kate as they took a seat each to face him across the desk.

"You've caught me at an extremely busy time, but let's not worry about that," he said as he retook his own seat. "Can I offer you some refreshment? Tea, perhaps? I've got every variety. Best bone china cups too. No rubbish."

"Thank you, but no," said Kate. "We won't be stopping long."

Ainsley signalled for his valet to leave before turning his attention back to his visitors – in particular, Kate.

"On the phone, you mentioned Lord Longbottom...?"

"We have a few things on our minds and were hoping you might be able to help us with them."

"Before I do, perhaps you can help me..."

He pointed to something in the corner behind them, forcing them to half-turn in their seats. On an easel was a medium-sized oil painting of an old ship.

"Very nice," said Kate.

"Perhaps Lady Jane could come over this evening to help me find the best place to hang it."

Kate and Jane turned instantly to Desmond Ainsley in shock.

"I'm busy," said Jane, recovering somewhat.

Ainsley sat back in his chair. "Pity…"

Kate wasn't impressed.

"I get the feeling you're used to getting your way in life."

"Ha! You should ask the owner of the Grosvenor Gallery in Brighton. That painting is by Allenby. Have you heard of him?"

Kate and Jane shook their heads.

Desmond grinned.

"Ladies, it's worth two hundred. I paid one-fifty. When Lord Longbottom visited the other day, he admired it greatly."

"Housebuilding plans?" said Jane. Her gaze was on the desk.

To Kate, it looked like an architect's drawing.

"Yes, I had a draughtsman in earlier. A few modifications to something I'm working on."

"At Ridgeway?" asked Jane.

"Yes, that's right."

"Where Simon Townsend hoped to build?" asked Kate.

Desmond Ainsley frowned.

"He may have had a word or two with the landowner, but that was long before I got involved."

"Are you aware that Lord Longbottom visited Simon Townsend last Friday?"

"No, but that's hardly any business of mine… or yours, for that matter. Now, tell me, Lady Jane. Did I hear you live in London?"

"Yes, in Mayfair."

"You know, I bet your house is full of fine paintings."

"One or two, perhaps."

"I get up to London quite often. I wouldn't be against popping in to see you. I could give you a few tips on acquiring the right kind of art for such a salubrious address."

Once again, Jane looked slightly nonplussed by Desmond Ainsley's outrageous modus operandi, but she took a steadying breath to recover the situation.

"Thanks for the offer, but there's no need. My brother, Alexander, lives there and is an art and antiquities expert… not to mention a firearms specialist."

"Ah."

Kate suppressed a smirk. While Jane's brother was no art and antiques expert, it was true about the firearms – him being an army officer.

"Well then, ladies," said Desmond through a somewhat strained grin, "you need my help…?"

"Lord Longbottom wanted the best for Sandham," said Kate. "He hated the thought of underhand practices ruining the town's reputation."

Desmond nodded. "And rightly so, Mrs Forbes. You'd be shocked at the sharp practices that go on all around us. It's a constant struggle to see that things are done properly.

On that score, Herbert and I were of one mind. He was certainly a great supporter of my Ridgeway scheme."

Kate felt like poking him in the eye but restrained herself.

"When you spoke to him at the town hall last night, did he mention anything that was troubling him?"

"Ladies, really, if this is some kind of makeshift investigation, you're wasting your time. The police have that chap Patterson in custody. He'll hang for his cowardly deed."

"Yes, but did Lord Longbottom say anything last night, or when you spoke with him the other day?"

"No, nothing of consequence. Now, if you'll excuse me, I'm very busy."

"Will you attend his memorial service?" asked Kate.

"Yes, of course. Mind you, there's trouble at the hall with the young members of that family. Don't let Miles fob you off."

"We've already spoken with him," said Kate.

"Yes, well, I must get on…"

Kate and Jane rose and bade him farewell. A moment later, they left the house with Kate feeling that Desmond Ainsley would be a tough nut to crack.

"He's pushing it a bit suggesting he was chums with Herbert."

"What's that, Aunt?" said Jane, almost laughing. "You mean you don't think Lord Longbottom was a supporter of Desmond Ainsley's honourable business practices?"

Kate knew full well her niece was joking – but even in jest, the idea rankled.

"I wonder what Fred Brigstock might have to say about it," she said as they got into the car.

Sixteen

Having negotiated a rough, bumpy stretch of country lane, Jane brought the Triumph to a halt at the Brigstock farmhouse gate.

"It's a good job the weather's dry," said Kate, "otherwise we'd be stuck in mud till next June."

The house itself was a ramshackle dirty white stucco affair with a thatched roof that had seen better days. There were also some large wooden outbuildings nearby whose purposes weren't immediately apparent.

As they tramped up to the front door, Kate spotted some cows in a far meadow. It was always a pleasing sight.

A moment later, she knocked.

And waited.

Then Jane pointed to a cross-field path between the house and some sheds fifty yards away. A large grey-haired woman in brown skirts and a grubby white apron was coming along it in their direction.

"You lost?" she called.

"We're looking for Mr Brigstock," replied Kate.

"You'll want the bottom then."

"Pardon me?"

"The bottom. He's repairing a fence in the bottom field."

"Ah… and which way is that?"

"No need. I'll get him for you."

If Kate had expected the woman to change direction – she didn't. She just kept heading for them, all the way until she brushed past them to reach the farmhouse door.

"Is it Mrs Brigstock?" asked Kate.

"That's right."

"I'm Mrs Forbes. This is my niece, Lady Jane Scott."

"I see."

"Your husband made a generous gesture last night about holding medieval re-enactments with horses and jousting in the meadow…"

"Forbes and Scott. I know those names. They say you interfere in other people's business."

"I can assure you our only interest is justice."

Mrs Brigstock went inside but returned almost immediately with a school bell, which she rang loudly just in front of Kate's face.

"He won't be a minute."

Indeed, a puffing Fred Brigstock soon appeared from the lane, although he didn't look too happy about it.

"Ladies…?"

"We're sorry to trouble you, Mr Brigstock," said Kate. "My niece, Lady Jane Scott and I have some concerns about Lord Longbottom's death. I wonder if you might be able to help us?"

He shrugged. "I don't see how. You saw what happened. The police nabbed that Patterson bloke. He'll be the one with all the answers."

"Interfering in other people's business…" muttered Mrs Brigstock as she went into the house.

Kate kept her attention on the husband.

"We spoke to Desmond Ainsley earlier about the Ridgeway housing scheme. Have you sold the land to him?"

Fred baulked. "That's private."

"His lordship was looking into a very serious matter. It may have related to the scheme."

"I'm sorry," said Fred, "but you're barking up the wrong tree. A lord of the realm wouldn't confide in the likes of me, and rightly so."

"Mr Brigstock, Lord Longbottom was murdered," said Jane. "If we can find out why, it might point to the culprit's identity."

"Sorry, my lady, but I don't recognize your authority."

Kate huffed. "Mr Brigstock, if you don't talk to us, you'll talk to Scotland Yard's man when we tell him of our concerns."

"That sounds like a threat," said Fred.

"It's not a threat. It's a fact."

Fred Brigstock thrust his hands into his pockets.

"There's no need for Scotland Yard's man to come here. I've done nothing wrong."

"Then there's no reason to avoid a simple question. Did you sell your land to Mr Ainsley?"

Fred pondered for a moment before grudgingly shaking his head.

"No, not yet. I've had a contract drawn up. It's not signed yet."

"We spoke to Simon Townsend," said Jane. "He wasn't very happy about the Ridgeway situation."

"Why would you talk to him?"

"He was your first housebuilding partner."

"It's my land. I'm free to do business with who I like."

Fred's discomfort was growing, so Kate pressed on.

"Did Lord Longbottom come to see you about it?"

"Yes, but…"

"What did you discuss?"

Fred sighed. "Townsend's plans didn't suit me, and so I thought that was an end to the houses being built. Then, out of the blue, Desmond Ainsley turned up with a more acceptable proposal. I explained all this to his lordship, and he left here satisfied."

"Are you sure Lord Longbottom was satisfied?" said Kate, feeling something to be amiss.

"Mr Ainsley made me a better offer. That's all. I've done nothing to warrant the interest of you or Scotland Yard."

"Well," said Kate, "as you say, there's nothing wrong in switching who you choose to deal with. Lord Longbottom had a bee in his bonnet about something, but it looks like we'll never know what."

"Right then. If that's all, some of us have work to do."

Kate nodded.

Before they could leave though, Mrs Brigstock emerged from the house and handed her a small crate filled with apples, pears, potatoes, carrots and a couple of cauliflowers.

"Oh!" said Kate.

She and Jane then thanked the Brigstocks and headed back to the car.

A moment later, pulling away from the farmhouse, Jane made an observation.

"Aunt, I think we've just been bribed."

Kate smiled but it didn't last.

"Are we barking up the wrong tree, Jane? We're supposed to be looking into the death of Herbert Longbottom and yet we seem to be knee-deep in a business spat instead."

"What do you want to do next then?"

"Make ourselves busy, Jane."

Seventeen

Kate experienced a dizzying hour as they tracked down their prey. First on their list was Mr Hilton, who Lord Longbottom had seen on the Monday before his demise. Although this was after the period when Herbert's mood darkened, the hope was that something might have been said.

As it was, Mr Hilton seemed surprised and then shocked to be the recipient of a visit. He maintained that his meeting with Lord Longbottom was to do with drainage, whereby one side of Hall Lane was prone to flooding in heavy rain. The solution, according to Mr Hilton, was to cut a channel and lay a pipe to get the water away. Although based in Sandham, Mr Hilton's expertise took him all over the south of England, so the business of entertaining summertime visitors held little personal interest for him – hence his absence from the function at the town hall.

Curiously, he had advised Simon Townsend on drainage by cesspit in relation to the Ridgeway project. It had been just a preliminary overview though. He'd heard nothing since.

Their second visit was to Mr Williams the upholsterer, who had only just returned from Haywards Heath and insisted that his lordship's serious concerns related to an armchair. He also seemed in a fret that he'd ordered material for a re-covering job which might not now go ahead – unless they cared to ask Miles Longbottom next time they saw him…?

Next, they decided to try Mr Swithin, the bank manager. However, approaching the Southern Counties building on the High Street, they came across Mr and Mrs Deane of the Coronation Dining Rooms – Mrs Deane being the woman who fainted at the site of Lord Longbottom's last moments.

"Mr and Mrs Deane, how are you?" asked Kate. "And Mrs Deane, are you sure you've recovered enough to be out and about?"

"I'm fine, Mrs Forbes. I went to the hospital as a precaution, but I didn't need to stay."

"No, she didn't need to stay," her husband repeated.

"Well, that's good to hear. This is my niece, Lady Jane Scott, by the way."

Mr Deane's eyes widened. "Lady Jane… hello."

"Hello," echoed Mrs Deane. "Are you investigating?"

"Hello to you too," said Jane with a disarming smile. "We're not investigating *as such* – we're more looking into events at the town hall. I know it must be difficult to think about, but has anything occurred to you regarding Lord Longbottom that, on reflection, might seem unusual?"

"No, sorry," said Mr Deane. "We've wondered about it, but we don't have any answers. It's a complete mystery why that chap did it."

"A complete mystery," repeated Mrs Deane.

"Lord Longbottom never hinted that anything was troubling him?"

"No, sorry."

"Well, we won't keep you," said Kate.

The Deanes continued along the High Street, leaving Kate and Jane at the bank entrance.

"Is one of them our killer, Jane?"

"Unless they stood to gain, then no. It doesn't seem likely that Lord Longbottom had any meaningful dealings with them."

Agreeing on this point, they entered the bank.

Fortunately, Mr Swithin had no appointments at the end of his working day and was willing to see them in his office. If they would just wait a few minutes outside…

Kate smiled but was frustrated. She wanted to get on with it so that she could go home and put her feet up.

"Chief Inspector Ridley," she mused as she adjusted her position on an uncomfortable chair. "I wonder how he's getting on."

"Hopefully, he's made some progress, Aunt."

"Hmm, let's hope he doesn't give up too easily."

Mr Swithin appeared at his office door and invited them in. A moment later they were seated and able to update him.

"Has Patterson not confessed yet?" he groaned from his large plain chair behind a large plain desk. "It would save a lot of pain for that poor family."

"No, he hasn't confessed," said Kate. "In the meantime, Jane and I are looking for anyone who saw or heard anything that might throw more light on what happened."

"Yes, well, as you know, I was at the town hall, but I'm not sure what more I can say."

"Something was troubling his lordship before his demise. You had lunch with him. Has anything occurred to you since? Anything that might help us?"

"No, sorry. At lunch, I could see he wasn't his usual self, which is why I engaged him with a number of entertaining anecdotes."

Kate almost winced.

"When did you first agree to have lunch?"

"Well… let me think… yes, we bumped into each other at a Chamber of Commerce function a couple of weeks ago. We didn't get much of a chance to speak though, so he thought a lunch appointment would be a good way to rectify it. He was a very sociable chap."

"Yes, he was. And his mood at the Chamber of Commerce get-together?"

"He was full of beans."

"Right."

"I'm sorry I can't help any more than that. Believe me, I wish I could."

"We're very grateful, Mr Swithin. Thank you for your time."

A moment later, they were back on the High Street in the sunshine.

"What now?" wondered Jane.

"Let's go home and rest for a bit," said Kate. "I'd like to be fresh for dinner at Pru and Christopher's."

Eighteen

That evening, a very short car journey brought Kate and Jane to Fairmile House in Burnt Ash Lane, where Jane parked the Triumph alongside the Davenports' Alvis tourer.

"Half-seven on the dot," said Kate, checking her watch.

Dinner with Sir Christopher and Lady Davenport would be at eight, giving them time for a catch up.

As it was, the catch up began no sooner they'd parked their backsides in the sitting room.

"Shocking," said Sir Christopher, brandishing the evening edition of the Sussex Chronicle newspaper. "Absolutely shocking!"

"Christopher's agitated," explained Pru.

The headline stated: 'Lord Longbottom Murdered in Sandham.'

Kate sighed. At least that part was factual.

"What do they say?" she asked.

Sir Christopher threw the paper down on the table.

"Apparently, *local sources* suggest Patterson harboured a grudge for years and, according to *reliable witnesses*, it was plain that death in a public place might not be mere happenstance."

Kate's nostrils flared.

"That's the work of Colin Nelson. He specializes in writing rubbish."

"Local sources, reliable witnesses," queried Jane. "I don't suppose any names are given?"

"Only one," said Sir Christopher. He picked the paper up again and scanned the newsprint. "Yes… it says Ernest Melton, the man in charge of the town hall's front door on the fateful night, fears a public display of fury on the streets of Sandham."

Kate growled. "The only display of public fury we'll have in Sandham will be me knocking on Ernie Melton's door."

"It doesn't look good for Robert Patterson though," said Pru.

"No, it doesn't," said Jane. "Unless we can uncover what was troubling Lord Longbottom, our investigation will remain stuck."

"Did you ladies not get far then?" asked Sir Christopher.

"Not as far as we'd have liked," said Kate.

"Herbert intended to discuss his problem with someone at the function," said Sir Christopher. "At least that narrows it down a bit."

"Unless they chose not to go," said Jane. "Simon Townsend stayed away and yet Lord Longbottom had been to see him."

"Herbert spoke with Miles," said Pru. "If I were that boy's parent, I'd certainly be troubled. He'd been in a fight, for goodness sake."

"Yes, I overheard part of their conversation," said Kate. "As I mentioned in my statement, Herbert told Miles that it was probably wise to not trouble the police. I've no idea what it was about though."

"Lord Longbottom had the family inventory out," said Jane. "I don't think we should jump to conclusions though. It could easily be unrelated."

Sir Christopher went to the window and peered into the dark.

"Desmond Ainsley," he said before turning to face the room.

"He's not in the garden, is he?" said Pru.

"No, I mean Herbert couldn't stand him – and they definitely had a word at the town hall."

"Herbert also spoke with Guy Royston and poor Mrs Deane," said Kate.

"But not Robert Patterson," said Sir Christopher.

"True," said Kate, "but we mustn't overlook the possibility that Robert Patterson just hadn't got around to it before the poisoning. The fact is we can't know for certain all those Herbert spoke to or intended to speak to."

"Who did you question today then?" asked Pru.

Kate took a breath. "Miles at Longbottom Hall, Simon Townsend at his building site in Holton, Desmond Ainsley at his house, and Fred Brigstock on his farm. We also spoke to Messrs Hilton and Williams, Mr and Mrs Deane, and Mr Swithin, none of whom can be viewed as suspicious."

"We also saw Mr and Mrs Royston," said Jane.

"At the school?" asked Sir Christopher.

"On the promenade by the tea rooms," said Kate. "They were out for a restorative walk. I can't say I've ever been to the school."

"Neither have I," said Sir Christopher, "although I hear it's a fine establishment. Now, my *alma mater*, that was a place and a half! The Sir Phillip Drew School for Boys. I often go back."

Pru rolled her eyes.

"Only because a certain former pupil's name is on a sporting honours board there."

"Yes, the one hundred yards dash! I was inspired that day."

Pru harrumphed. "I heard someone let a bull in through the gate by the starting line."

"Getting back to All Saints," said Jane, "did Lord Longbottom have any connection to the school beyond his sons' attendance there?"

"Yes, Herbert's father, Arthur, was a trustee when it first opened. Herbert would occasionally talk about the rushing around his father did to help get it ready: drumming up donations of everything from chairs to crockery, loans of anything they could get their hands on… I believe he and Lady Rushton sat up half the night for weeks writing the curriculum. Er, not in the same room, of course!"

"I'm assuming she's no longer with us," said Jane.

"Alas, she popped off quite some time ago."

"But the Longbottoms knew the Rushtons well."

"Well, it's ancient history now, but I gather Arthur paid for a couple of scholarships as a charitable donation and persuaded a shotgun-wielding farmer along the road to sell the school a plot of land to create the rugby pitches. Both Arthur and Herbert were very fine men."

"And now we have Miles," said Pru in a non-committal way.

"Lord Longbottom was due to visit the school next Monday," said Jane.

"A drinkies thing?" queried Sir Christopher. "I didn't hear about that."

"No, according to his appointment diary, he was due there at nine o'clock on Monday morning."

"At the school?" Sir Christopher was shaking his head. "He loved attending the fete, sports day, prize-giving and so on, but nine o'clock Monday morning sounds too formal for Herbert."

Pru shrugged. "I hope we can resolve this rotten business before the memorial service."

Sir Christopher brightened. "Speaking of resolving things…"

They watched him skip over to a far corner of the room, where a white sheet covered his crime board. However, when he pulled the sheet away, there were two boards, one behind the other, both on easels – the second of which he placed alongside the first.

"Two chalkboards?" queried Kate.

"I remembered there was a second one in the loft. Not that I'm happy. While rooting around up there, I realised that Eric was missing."

"Eric?"

"His toy train," said Pru.

"Eric is not a train, he's an engine who pulls a train. Except he can't in this household because both he and his two carriages were sold off without my knowledge."

Pru rolled her eyes. "They weren't sold off. I gave them to the children's hospital in Brighton ten years ago."

"Yes, well, getting back to the business of suspects," said a disheartened Sir Christopher, "I'll add Simon Townsend and Mrs Deane to the left-hand board. And Mr Deane too, for good measure…"

There was a knock at the sitting room door followed by the appearance of Fossett.

"Chief Inspector Ridley is here. He wonders if he might have a word."

"Show him in!" exclaimed Sir Christopher.

A moment later, Ridley entered the room, hat in one hand, a briefcase in the other.

"I never heard a car?" queried Pru.

"I walked from the police station, Lady Davenport. A very pleasant fifteen minutes. I even spotted an owl looking for prey."

Sir Christopher laughed. "Just like you, eh chief inspector!"

"Yes, well… just to let you know that I must formally charge Robert Patterson with Lord Longbottom's murder."

"Fingerprints?" asked Jane.

"Only his lordship's – but we have enough to get cracking. That said, I have something in mind regarding the case…"

"You've come to the right place, old boy," said Sir Christopher, luring Ridley to the twin chalkboards.

While Ridley was distracted, Kate made animated gestures to Pru, who could only frown in response. A frustrated Kate then held an imaginary knife and fork and acted out eating food, while pointing at the chief inspector's back.

Finally, the penny dropped.

"Chief Inspector," said Pru, "you must join us for dinner."

Ridley turned, looking surprised.

"Oh, I wouldn't want to put you to any trouble."

"It's a capital idea," insisted Sir Christopher. "You must stay!"

Kate and Jane smiled warmly, causing Ridley to emit a resigned sigh.

"Yes, alright then. Why not. Thanks very much."

Nineteen

The Davenports and their guests took their seats in the dining room, while Fossett poured each a glass of claret.

"The onion soup will be five minutes," he announced before departing.

"Did you have any luck with Miles Longbottom?" Kate asked the chief inspector. "We saw him but it's possible he might have held back on us."

"Yes, I saw him. He agreed that something was troubling his father, but he reckons nothing tangible was said about it. I mentioned what you overheard. He wasn't happy about that. He said it was a problem with a servant at his London address. Apparently, a low-value trinket went missing."

"Ah," said Kate. "That explains it then."

"What meals do they serve at the police station, Chief Inspector?" asked Pru.

"Oh… young Edmonds is staying overnight while there's a prisoner. I expect he'll make them both a cheese and ham sandwich. Anything more complicated and Edmonds would probably burn the station down."

"Poor Mr Patterson must be worried sick," said Pru.

Sir Christopher shook his head.

"It's always a rotten business when an ex-army man gets a bad name."

"If Robert Patterson is guilty," said Kate, "then that's where the trouble started."

"Yes," said Ridley, "a man died due to silly high jinks and Patterson was one of those who took the blame. He swears it's all in the past though. Of course, a jury will most likely decide otherwise."

"I don't suppose you served in the armed forces during the War, Chief Inspector?" said Sir Christopher.

"No, I was promoted to detective sergeant just before the War. I did raise the possibility of volunteering but got short shrift from Chief Superintendent Tippett."

"What did he say?" wondered Pru.

Ridley glanced around the dinner table, clearly mindful of mixed company.

"Something along the lines of: 'Are you expecting all the criminals to take a rest, you silly man.' Words to that effect."

"So, you remained at Scotland Yard," said Kate.

"Yes, and the Chief Super was right. The criminals didn't take a break. That's to say, while a fair few of the younger ones went off to war, the middling and older ones stepped in to plug the gap."

"The rotters," said Sir Christopher.

"I started as a policeman in London in 1904, and not a day's gone by where there hasn't been a crime. It's the busiest business you'll ever come across."

"What was the first crime you encountered?" asked Kate.

"Oh… well… that would be a drunken chap causing trouble in King Street, Hammersmith. He thought smashing a couple of beer bottles in the street was a perfectly acceptable activity."

"And what about your first job as a detective?"

"Ah… a murder in Notting Hill. You don't mind me mentioning more murder at the dinner table? I wouldn't want to put anyone off their onion soup."

"No, carry on," said Pru.

"I hope it's not too shocking," said Sir Christopher.

"For whose sake?" asked Pru.

"Well, for the sake of…" Sir Christopher took stock of those present – his formidable wife and the celebrated sleuths, Kate Forbes and Lady Jane Scott. "Er… carry on, Chief Inspector."

"Don't worry, Sir Christopher. This was a fiendish plot involving a stolen wallet."

"Jolly good. Crack on then!"

"Well, I was a fresh-faced detective constable, and my inspector was a chap called Wilton – a man of great experience and not far off retirement. I worked under him on my first twenty or so cases and learned quite a bit."

"How exciting," said Pru.

"The first was the theft of a wallet that involved murder. A chap was found dead near Notting Hill Gate and he had this wallet on him. We didn't have to wait long before another chap turned up claiming the wallet was his and that this ruffian had stolen it. The question was – how did the dead man with the wallet meet his end? The theory was that another crook saw what had happened and decided to take advantage by bashing the wallet thief over the head. Unfortunately, before he could take the wallet for himself, members of the public shouted and came running, meaning this second felon had to flee empty-handed. The victim of the original wallet theft was relieved. He'd at least get his money back. When we interviewed him, he didn't seem too bothered about the dead man. Anyway, I thought I'd test the strength of his claim on the wallet by asking how much was in it."

"Oh, very good," said Sir Christopher.

"Well, he had the amount right. It was ninety pounds. The thing was – he failed to mention the newspaper clipping folded up inside it."

Kate's eyes widened.

"I didn't see that coming."

"Well, Inspector Wilton called me to one side and asked what I thought of this chap and his wallet. He made me think of alternative scenarios, just to make sure we weren't giving a substantial amount of money to the wrong man and letting him walk away."

"What ruse did you come up with?" asked Sir Christopher.

"One idea I had was this. What if this fellow had owed the dead man ninety pounds. And what if he'd paid him the money. And what if he'd seen the chap put the money in the wallet, which he'd have noticed didn't contain any other bank notes."

"Very plausible," said Sir Christopher.

"Christopher, shush," said Pru.

Kate frowned.

"Chief Inspector, are you suggesting the wallet theft victim was the killer?"

"Yes, I am, but there were no witnesses who could definitely identify him, so we were on the verge of handing the wallet over."

"Regarding the wallet," said Jane. "Were there any identifying features?"

"Nope – it was just a tatty, brown thing."

"What happened next?" said a wide-eyed Pru.

"Well, I told this chap he could have the wallet and the money. He looked very excited, I can tell you. He even reached out for me to hand it over. Then I said he just had to do one thing for me. Tell me the contents of the newspaper clipping. He couldn't, of course. It wasn't his wallet. He complained he'd not read the clipping, but it was a well-thumbed section on rooms to let, so that was a lie.

Solely because of this, I spent days and days trying to find a connection between the killer and the victim. And eventually I did. They were tied by a gambling connection. This proved they knew each other. The jury agreed and he met his end. Inspector Wilton said if I kept at it, I might make a good detective."

"Bravo," said Sir Christopher. "You know I sometimes think I missed my vocation by not working for Scotland Yard."

Pru coughed. "Yes dear."

"Thing is, the story's not finished," said Ridley. "Seven years later, at Inspector Wilton's retirement party, I reminded him of the wallet murder case. Well, blow me down if he didn't smile and say that planting the newspaper clipping in the wallet had been a good day's work on his part."

"My goodness me," said Pru. "Your old boss was as fiendish as the crooks!"

"Yes, he was. It taught me something though. As a police detective, it's my duty to see that justice is done by using all fair means available to me. But I won't rule out, as a last resort, reluctantly... well..."

"Allowing a murderer to trap themselves?" suggested Jane.

"Yes, well put, Lady Jane. There are evil men and women out there. Sometimes, justice needs a helping hand."

Twenty

After dinner, the company adjourned to various seats in the drawing room, where the men enjoyed cigars while Pru opted for a cigarette in a sleek silver holder. All had a nip of brandy.

"So how does one get promoted at Scotland Yard?" asked Sir Christopher.

"Luck," said Ridley.

"Surely not."

"Well, in fairness, there's a bit more to it. Skill, endeavour, tenacity… but, yep, luck helps. There are good detectives who don't get a break in big cases, while others get lucky. Mind you, some of the bone-headed variety often snooker themselves with a know-all attitude. Not that we have many of those, of course."

"It certainly doesn't apply to you," said Kate, perched on the edge of a red leather wingback armchair.

"Thanks, Mrs Forbes. My bosses picked up on that. They said I was good at working with witnesses to gain extra insight."

Pru put her glass down. "You mean Kate and Jane have helped you get promoted?"

Ridley's eyes widened. "I wouldn't go that far. That said, yes, Mrs Forbes and Lady Jane have a way about them. I'd be a fool to discount their findings or their views."

"We've not been helpful in this latest case though," lamented Kate.

"On the contrary, you've had a word with a few witnesses and haven't managed to find an alternative explanation for what happened. That, in itself, is useful."

"We'll keep trying," said Kate. "Even though you'll soon be back in London."

"Obviously, if you learn anything, contact me at the Yard."

"Who did Mr Patterson speak to at the function?" asked Jane.

Ridley rested his cigar in the nearby ashtray.

"Just to be clear, I would never divulge what's in a statement to you. However, if an innocent man's life is in danger… I'll just get my case."

Ridley left for the sitting room and returned with his briefcase. He took a seat near Jane and placed the case on the coffee table to open it.

He then pulled out some papers and sifted through to find what he wanted. The others he set down on the open case. Reading from Patterson's statement, he paraphrased for his audience.

"Patterson says he received an invitation from Lord Longbottom…" Ridley took the invitation and placed it uppermost on the pile. "Then he attended the get-together where he spoke with Mrs Forbes, and then with Fred Brigstock and Desmond Ainsley, then Mr Deane of the Coronation Dining Rooms. He says he was alone when Lord Longbottom collapsed."

"Aunt Kate?" asked Jane. "Over at Holton, we were discussing Mr Patterson being accused of murder. Can you recall your thoughts on how he'd be feeling about attending the town hall function?"

Kate took a moment.

"Only that he probably wished he'd never been invited."

Jane turned to Ridley.

"Chief Inspector, are you aware that Mr Patterson's invitation differs from my aunt's?"

Ridley stared down at the card.

"Does it?"

Jane seemed quite certain. "The handwriting lacks fluidity, as if someone has very carefully replicated an original card. Aunt, is yours still on your mantlepiece?"

"With Ernie Melton on the door at the town hall? No, I took it with me. Which means…" She retrieved her handbag from the floor beside the armchair and had a rummage. "I really must have a major clear out. This bag holds more items than the British Museum, and I'm sure some of them are just as old."

She extracted the card. It wasn't glitzy; more an everyday item. The large, central, printed heading stated: 'Invitation'. Beneath this, to the left, were four more printed words with a suitable space allocated to each: 'To', 'From', 'Date', and 'Venue'. These details had been entered by pen in blue ink. Finally, in the bottom right corner, was a printed 'R.S.V.P.' to which Herbert had added: Longbottom Hall.

Kate passed it to Ridley, who compared it with the Patterson invitation. He spent a few moments before shaking his head.

"Well, I'll be…"

"Here's ours," said Pru, having gone through her own bag.

Ridley compared this one too.

"Lady Davenport, yours and Mrs Forbes' invitations are identical. The one Patterson received though… it's as Lady Jane says – a clever forgery."

Sir Christopher got up and began pacing.

"Are we saying that someone pretending to be Herbert Longbottom sent Mr Patterson a dodgy invite?"

"Yes, we are," said Jane.

Pru rolled her cigarette holder between her thumb and forefinger.

"What will you do, Chief Inspector?"

Ridley frowned.

"Well, Patterson might have set himself up, Lady Davenport. You know, as a clever ruse."

Sir Christopher's eyes narrowed.

"A clever ruse, eh?"

"I don't think so," said Jane.

"I'm inclined to agree," sighed Ridley.

"So am I," said Sir Christopher.

"Do we know when the invitations went out?" asked Jane.

"Initially, two weeks ago," said Kate. "The response wasn't quite what Herbert hoped for though, so he sent out some more a few days ago."

Jane nodded. "Do we know when Mr Patterson received his invitation?"

"It's in his statement," said Ridley, already studying the document. "It was the morning of the function. He was at work, so he didn't know until a message reached him from his mother. That was at lunchtime."

"Very handy," said Pru. "Such a late invitation wouldn't have given him much opportunity to bump into Lord Longbottom."

Sir Christopher took his seat again.

"Whoever set him up is clearly a devious operative."

Pru rolled her eyes.

"That narrows it down to half the Chamber of Commerce plus next door's cat."

Kate looked to Ridley.

"Someone has murdered our friend and set Robert Patterson up to take the blame. You can't go back to London."

Ridley seemed to ponder it.

"Look, I'm staying at the Prince of Wales pub near the quayside. Scotland Yard expenses don't stretch to the Crown Hotel, more's the pity. Anyway, I'll extend my stay an extra night."

"I wonder what your superiors will think," said Jane.

"Well, the Chief Constable of Sussex wants it resolved pronto – something he's sure to mention to his pal, the Commissioner of the Metropolitan Police, which means my boss at the Yard getting a hefty nudge and me getting it in the neck. I dunno… just as I was getting to enjoy my promotion. Oh well, easy come, easy go."

"Oh, it's not that serious," said Pru. "I'm sure your long years of service will be taken into account."

"Hmm…" huffed Ridley as he slid the various invitations and other papers into his case. "If Robert Patterson *was* set up, we need to find out fast who did it."

Kate raised an eyebrow.

"You said 'we'…?"

"Yes, keep your eyes and ears open. If the Chief Constable decides that Patterson created his own invitation just to get into the function, it won't be long before my bosses at the Yard hear about it."

"It might be best if news of the counterfeit invitation is held back from the other suspects," said Jane.

"Agreed," said Ridley.

"Right then," said Kate. "First thing tomorrow, we have work to do."

Twenty-One

Kate was sitting on the edge of her bed, washed, dressed and ready to go down for a hearty breakfast. She could already hear Jane moving around downstairs. There was just the small matter of the unsent letter sitting on her dressing table. The one she was supposed to post to Peregrine Nash.

What to do?

She roused herself and went to join Jane.

Ten minutes later, they were enjoying coffee, kippers and toast at the dining table.

"We have a lot of work to do today," said Jane.

"We do," said Kate. "Are we still united in our belief that Robert Patterson is most likely innocent?"

"We are."

"And we don't believe he wrote the invitation himself, just to gain entry to the town hall?"

"We don't. He could have bashed Lord Longbottom over the head on a dark night. There's also the matter of the counterfeit invitation card having been copied. Patterson would have given himself the secondary problem of obtaining a genuine one to copy from."

Kate nodded. "Yes, our killer was someone with a genuine invitation card. Desmond Ainsley, for example."

"This is no time for wishful thinking, Aunt."

"Well, *all* those at the event with a link to Herbert then. Miles Longbottom, for example."

"A son in a fight; a troubled father. There's more to it than Miles is letting on. I wonder what his brother makes of it all."

"Ian? He's certainly an elusive one."

"Then there's a deal between Fred Brigstock and your dear friend, Desmond Ainsley that replaced a deal between Fred and Simon Townsend."

"I wouldn't blame Mr Townsend for committing murder," said Kate, "but I'd have thought it would be against Desmond Ainsley rather than Herbert."

"Mr Townsend wasn't at the function," Jane pointed out. "Neither was Ian. And yet, in both cases, there's the possibility of a collaboration with someone who was."

"Hmm… there's also the business of Guy Royston and his appointment with Herbert."

"Yes, arranged for next Monday. That's worth a bit more thought. What about Mr and Mrs Deane? Are we right to rule them out?"

"I'm sure Herbert had no meaningful dealings with them. That said, Mr Deane spoke with Herbert, and of course Mrs Deane was at his side when…"

"Yes… anyone else?"

Kate let out a sigh. "Perry Nash…"

"Pardon?"

"Oh… sorry. Not a suspect."

"What's up?"

"We're meant to be having lunch at the Crown tomorrow."

"Yes, I know."

"He wrote to me to confirm it."

"I know that too, Aunt. You're all set for a lovely get-together."

"I wrote another letter to confirm that I'd received his confirmation."

"That's probably too much."

"I didn't send it."

"Oh? Why not?"

"The vicar's wife."

"Don't tell me she stole it."

"She was at the post office just as I was about to post it. She asked how long it was since I lost Henry. At that moment, I felt pure guilt, because it's sixteen months, Jane. No time at all."

Jane got up and came round to Kate's side of the table, where she placed her hand on her aunt's shoulder.

"You're being too hard on yourself."

"I could never be disrespectful to Henry's memory."

"You're not. Far from it."

"Then why do I feel upset?"

"I'm not really qualified to give you advice. It's always been the other way round."

"I know, but I just feel a little lost right now."

Jane pulled the nearest chair round so that they could sit side by side.

"Aunt, somebody once told me that as we get older we're prone to becoming more certain about things; sometimes to the point where we stop listening to other perspectives."

"You're describing Parliament, Jane."

"It was Professor Peregrine Nash who told me that. He was talking about certain senior colleagues at Oxford University."

"I expect he was making sure you'll always keep an open mind."

"He was, and he still does. He's a good man, Aunt Kate. One of the very best."

"I get that feeling too."

"Alright, my opinion then. Uncle Henry would want you to be happy. In fact, I'll go further. He'd be upset if you chose to live unhappily in his name."

Kate thought of her husband. She could picture him smiling.

"I suppose you're right."

"You don't have to change your thoughts on Perry Nash for *anyone*. You're right about sixteen months not being a long time. For you to marry the professor next week would definitely be too soon. But for you two to progress to something meaningful over a longer period – another year or two, for example…"

From her bag, Kate retrieved Perry's letter and the one she had failed to send in response. The first of these, she read aloud to Jane.

> Dear Kate,
>
> I'm very much looking forward to our lunch date on Saturday. I'll be arriving at Sandham Station at 11:20. It was very kind of you to offer to pick me up from there. Thank you.
>
> Until Saturday.
>
> Fondest regards,
>
> Perry

She put the letter down and picked up her unsent reply.

"This is the one I wrote in response after speaking with the vicar's wife."

> Dear Professor,
>
> I'll meet you at the station as arranged.
>
> Lunch will be at the Crown Hotel. One o'clock.
>
> Yours sincerely,
>
> Kate Forbes

Kate noticed Jane wince but said nothing. However, her niece smiled when Kate tore it in half.

"It's a bit late to send anything now."

"Write it anyway."

"Pardon?"

"Go on, write the version you'd love to send."

Kate laughed for a brief moment but stopped herself.

"Alright."

She would respond with dignity and respect for her late husband… and with hope for the future. It was a difficult balance to get right, but she would do her best. A moment later, at the dining room table, she wrote:

> Dear Perry,
>
> Thank you for confirming Saturday's arrangements for lunch at the Crown. I'm also very much looking forward to it.
>
> Gertie and I will meet you as arranged.
>
> Warmest regards,
>
> Kate

She read it aloud to Jane, who nodded.

"Now tuck that away, Aunt, and use its tone for your greeting when you meet."

"You approve then?"

"As your loving niece, yes, I approve."

"And as my friend?"

"Oh... as your friend, I'm beyond delighted. I think the sooner you two kiss, the better.

Kate laughed. She then savoured the moment.

"Ahh, I feel a lot better, Jane."

"That's what friends are for."

Their shared smile warmed Kate's heart.

"Right then," she said, feeling they really ought to get the day started. "Where should we venture first?"

"I'd say we've already spoken to the killer. And Lord Longbottom didn't trust Desmond Ainsley. How about we let Mrs Patterson know there's hope and then apply a little pressure to Mr Ainsley. Hopefully that veneer of respectability might be thin enough to crack."

Twenty-Two

As planned, their first stop was a small white thatched cottage in Long Lane, home to Mrs Patterson. Pulling up outside, Kate noticed the newness of the sturdy front door. No doubt courtesy of the occupant's carpenter son.

They weren't consulting detectives, of course, but Mrs Patterson had wanted them to act as such for her son's sake and had offered to pay them. It seemed only right they should report their findings to her.

As it was, Mrs Patterson was at the front door before they got out of the car.

"Mrs Forbes! What a marvel you are!"

Clearly, news travelled fast.

"My niece is the marvel – Lady Jane Scott."

"My lady." Mrs Patterson half-curtsied then showed them in. "Can I offer you some refreshment?"

"No, thank you," said Kate. "We can't stop long."

A moment later, they were seated in a tiny front room with faded mismatched chairs, a worn rug, but a new sideboard and plenty of coal on the fire.

"I saw Sergeant Jones," said Mrs Patterson, "so I know the latest. I'd just like to thank you for helping to set the record straight for my Robert."

"We're doing all we can," said Jane, "But there's more to be done if we're to clear his name."

"Were you able to see him?" asked Kate.

"Just for a few minutes. He looks well, but he's in the dark about the whole thing, poor lamb."

"I can only imagine," said Kate.

"You know, you really must let me pay you for your efforts, Mrs Forbes."

"No, Jane and I will be happy to see justice done. That's reward enough."

"A piece of seed cake then. Fresh from the baker this morning."

"Very well then. Thank you."

Mrs Patterson disappeared for a moment and returned with a small piece of cake on small plates for all three of them.

Kate took a bite.

"Mmm, lovely."

It didn't take long to get through the cakes – three bites for Kate – and then it was back to business.

"Any ideas, Mrs Patterson? Anything that can strengthen your son's defence?"

"No, but surely this new evidence should make all the difference."

"Did the sergeant tell you the nature of the new evidence?"

"No, he mentioned your involvement, but he wouldn't say what it was. He reckons your Scotland Yard friend wants to keep the real killer guessing."

"Yes, no doubt," said Kate. "The thing is, your son isn't out of the woods yet. There's still a possibility of it going to court on the basis that he set himself up to wrong-foot the police."

Mrs Patterson shrugged it off with a short, abrupt laugh.

"Rubbish!" she snorted.

"We agree," said Kate, "but there it is. It could still go to court."

"We'll keep at it, Mrs Patterson," said Jane. "That much you can rely on."

A few minutes later, they were driving away.

Twenty-Three

Out on the northeast edge of Sandham, Jane brought the Triumph to a halt outside Ainsley House. Behind closed gates, Desmond Ainsley's Rolls-Royce Phantom sat on the drive with a seagull's deposit on the shiny bonnet, suggesting Desmond was at home and that his valet had an unpleasant job awaiting him.

"You said he was rude to Uncle Henry."

Kate growled. "He asked how much it would cost to influence a trial."

"I assume it was a general inquiry rather than a specific case."

"More a boast that he's beyond the reach of the law. To think he's about to start building homes in Sandham. There's bound to be foul play involved."

"Er... wishful thinking, Aunt?"

"Sorry, I can't help it."

They got out of the car and walked through the pedestrian gate to the arched doorway.

"I preferred it when this was The Brambles," said Kate before knocking.

A moment later, they were met with a quizzical look from Ainsley's valet.

"Good morning. It's Mrs Forbes and Lady Jane Scott again. We'd like to speak with Mr Ainsley."

The valet bowed slightly.

"I'll see if he's available."

Once again, they were left standing on the doorstep until the valet returned.

"Mr Ainsley will see you in the sitting room. This way, please."

They passed through the expensively decorated hallway, averted their gaze from Ainsley's portrait, and arrived at the next door along from their previous visit.

The valet knocked and pushed it open. He then stood aside to let them into a large sitting room that, like the study, overlooked the garden. Here, a baby grand piano took up one corner, while the rest of the room boasted a fine stone fireplace, two luxurious sofas and two armchairs, while the walls were adorned with a variety of English countryside oil paintings and fancy mirrors. Two bold red rugs augmented the polished oak floor while a few shaded electric lamps would no doubt bring the place to life after dark.

"Your visitors, Mr Ainsley."

Dressed in yet another fine suit, Desmond Ainsley was at one of the windows surveying his garden. He turned once the valet had announced the arrivals.

"Ah… we meet again."

He signalled for his valet to leave without bothering to see if his visitors required refreshment. Neither did he offer them a seat.

"We won't stop," said Kate. "We still have a thing or two on our minds and wondered if you might help us clear them up."

"I don't see how, but feel free to ask anyway."

"Fred Brigstock had an arrangement with Simon Townsend, but something happened to make Mr Brigstock pull out."

Desmond waved a dismissive hand.

"Yes, I've heard all the rot about mean, nasty Desmond Ainsley coming along like the big bad wolf. The fact is, I offered Mr Brigstock a better deal, which he accepted."

Jane stirred. "Why would Lord Longbottom look into such an innocuous affair?"

Desmond slowly shook his head.

"Lord Longbottom was looking into Simon Townsend's dealings, not mine. If there's something amiss, I suggest you look into Townsend's business methods. Unless he's a friend of yours…?"

"We're looking into a matter of murder," said Kate. "As tempting as it might be, we're not for or against anyone when it comes to housebuilding."

"Well, if you're keeping an open mind, you might consider that Townsend attempted to recruit his lordship to look into something he wished to overturn. I think the phrase is sour grapes. As far as I know, Lord Longbottom merely asked a question or two before dismissing Townsend's views as fanciful."

"We don't know he dismissed Mr Townsend's views."

"This is all nonsense, ladies. A lord of the realm is dead and you're looking into a matter that will never produce a motive for murder however much you pry. On top of which, the police have their man."

Kate fixed him with her steadiest gaze.

"We believe Robert Patterson is innocent."

Desmond laughed.

"I'm sorry, but what you believe is of little consequence."

"Chief Inspector Ridley of Scotland Yard accepts that Robert is no longer the only suspect. He changed his mind last night, while we were having dinner with him."

For a brief moment Desmond appeared to gnash his teeth, but a broad grin was quickly in place.

"May I ask *why* he changed his mind?"

"We're not at liberty to say. Now, why don't you tell us when you first approached Fred Brigstock. Are you sure it was after Simon Townsend's deal fell through? Or was it while that deal was going ahead. And before you answer, be aware that we're planning to discuss it with both the chief inspector *and* Fred Brigstock."

Desmond took a breath.

"Well, now… let me think… yes, I may have bumped into Fred while the Townsend deal was being put together. Just a friendly chat, you know. Old friends and all that."

"How long have you and Fred been friends then?"

"Oh… years. Now, if you'll excuse me, time and tide wait for no man, and I really must be getting on with my day."

"Very well."

Shadowed by Ainsley's valet, they departed with Kate feeling they hadn't made enough progress – unless the objective had been to confirm that Desmond Ainsley was deeply untrustworthy.

"What next?" she said as they reached the gate.

Just then, Desmond appeared on the doorstep.

"Just one thing…"

They turned to face him.

"What's that?"

He shooed his valet away and waited a moment, even coming a few steps along the path.

"I shouldn't say this, but yesterday, when I mentioned there being a problem at Longbottom Hall…? It's gambling debts."

"Why are you telling us this?" snapped Kate. To her it sounded like malicious gossip.

But Desmond Ainsley merely shrugged.

"It's useful to learn as much as possible about the people we move amongst. Knowledge is power."

"You must have some very low people assisting you, Mr Ainsley," said Kate.

"No comment."

"Gambling debts?" mused Jane.

"Yes," said Ainsley. "If Lord Longbottom had something serious on his mind, that might have been it. By the way, you never heard it from me."

Twenty-Four

Jane drove them towards Longbottom Hall under a clear blue sky and, for a time, behind a great red traction engine whose driver seemed to believe he had exclusive rights to the middle of the road.

Jane resisted the temptation to roar past him at the first opportunity and instead overtook slowly with a friendly wave. Kate's thoughts were elsewhere though. On murder and mendacity.

"Such a lovely day, and such a miserable business," she observed.

"Yes, it is. We'll do our best though."

"Yes, we will." Kate brightened a little. "I still think of the old days at the hall."

"Those long lunches?"

"Yes, those *very* long lunches." Kate smiled, but it didn't last. "I wonder if Miles will be pleased to see us again."

"I'd say not, Aunt. We're rattling cages."

"Hmm, rattling cages at a time Miles inherits money and a title."

"Not to mention at a time he has a bruise on his face and there's gossip of gambling debts."

"I wouldn't like to say what I think about that. Was the motive for murder to get the inheritance to pay off the debts? It seems so rotten. Then again, gambling is a curse that forces sane people into terrible situations. And let's not forget he has a wife and two children in London. What must they have made of him bumping into a cupboard door?"

As before, Jane drove through the open gates and along the short drive up to the large Georgian house, where she pulled over by a freestanding garage. The Silver Ghost was outside with a member of the Longbottom family standing beside it.

"Hello, Ian," said Kate as she got out of the Triumph.

Herbert's second son offered a thin smile.

"Hello, Mrs Forbes. How lovely to see you."

"I'm so sorry for your loss. Your father was a fine man."

"Thank you."

"It's been such a long while since we last met. Let me introduce my niece, Lady Jane Scott."

Ian turned to Jane, who had also stepped out of the car.

"Lady Jane, a pleasure. Please do call me Ian."

"Ian, thank you. It seems our paths have never crossed."

"No, I'd have remembered if they had."

"I didn't know your father, but you have my sympathies."

"Thank you."

It occurred to Kate that in Victorian times, a meeting between the son of a baron and the daughter of an earl would have people saying one plus one equals marriage, but this was 1928 – the peak of Modern Times and Jane had a mind of her own and a chap in London who was currently leafing through old books in a library. While Harry wasn't from noble stock, he was a fine young man and one Kate would be very happy to welcome into the family – should Jane decide on it.

"I hear you're looking into the matter of my father's death," said Ian.

"That's right," said Kate.

"But the police have the culprit."

"Perhaps not," said Jane. "A degree of doubt has crept in."

"Oh?" Ian's demeanour changed. "What kind of doubt?"

"There's a possibility that someone else poisoned your father and tried to place the blame on an innocent man."

Ian shook his head in disbelief.

"Are there any suggestions as to this devil's identity?"

"Not yet," said Kate, "but Jane and I are asking questions of a number of those who were present at the function. If we learn anything of use, we'll inform Chief Inspector Ridley immediately."

"The Scotland Yard man. A friend of yours, I hear."

"Hardly a friend," said Kate, "but our paths have crossed."

"Well then," said Ian, "that means you're either here to give my family a progress report, or you're here to question my brother."

"Perhaps both," said Jane. "You and Miles came back to Sandham together. Miles returned for the town hall function. Are you able to say why you returned?"

"Me? You surely don't suspect me. I wasn't even at the rotten event. No offence, Mrs Forbes."

"None taken."

"I came back because… it was high time I saw my father and sister. Six months in London is too long without visiting one's family. I only wished I'd come back sooner."

"Yes, of course," said Kate, sympathetically.

Ian shifted his weight from one foot to the other and back again.

"Does the same apply to Miles?" asked Jane. "Is he a rare visitor?"

"No, Miles pops back all the time. Only, this time he was called back because Father wanted him to head up a summertime economy committee."

Kate nodded. "The function at the town hall was to test the level of interest. Your father was hopeful we'd soon have Miles leading the way."

"It all sounds quite innocent to me," said Ian. "Miles certainly had no motive to commit murder."

Kate's stare was unwavering.

"An urgent need to repay a debt might be a motive."

Ian's face flushed. "A debt? Where did you get such an idea?"

The front door of the house creaked open.

"I'd like to know that too," said Miles, who had clearly been listening.

"Ah, Miles," said Kate. "I'm sorry to be so blunt, but I think the pleasantries can be set aside for now. Do you have gambling debts?"

Miles bristled as he came over to join them.

"Whoever told you that is a stirrer. I also have no idea why you're asking."

"They don't think it's Patterson," said Ian.

"Oh?"

"New evidence," said Jane.

"What new evidence?"

"They won't say," said Ian.

"It's a police matter," said Kate. "Jane discovered something that Scotland Yard are taking seriously. It's possible that someone killed your father and set Patterson up to take the blame."

Miles sighed.

"I see…"

"Chief Inspector Ridley will no doubt call on you."

"Yes, well, it's a shock to hear it might be someone other than Patterson, but there are no motives for murder at Longbottom Hall."

Ian stirred. "Have you spoken with all those our father spoke to?"

"Yes, we believe so, along with those we believe he intended to speak to. But none of that matters if they had no opportunity to upset him between Friday morning and Sunday morning. Miles, you returned to Sandham with a bruised face. Are you certain it wasn't connected to the serious business troubling your father?"

Miles opened the driver's door of the Rolls-Royce and got in.

"I've already explained how I walked into a cupboard door. It could happen to anyone. Now, if you don't mind, Ian and I have some private business to attend to."

Ian shrugged and got into the car.

Kate wondered. Miles now gained the Longbottom estate, and he had the opportunity to commit the crime. To risk his neck for something he would get anyway meant it had to be an act of desperation. Perhaps this was one for Ridley to look into.

Through the window, Miles smiled as the engine fired up.

"I'm having a few people here tomorrow afternoon at three to discuss my father's commemoration plans. You should both come along."

The Rolls-Royce pulled away before Kate could answer.

"Ian's a strange one," said Jane as she opened the driver's door of the Triumph.

Just then, Helen came outside.

"I heard what my brothers said…"

"Then you know it's all up the air," said Kate.

"Look, whatever the truth is, however bad, I want it to come out."

"Is there something on your mind then?"

"Well…" Helen sighed with frustration. "I spoke to Craven, our butler. He said that Father made a telephone call to London… to Miles… on Saturday."

"I see," said Kate.

"He says it was the only incoming or outgoing call of the time I was away. I don't know if the conversation with Miles is what put my father in a bad mood. Craven would never listen in, so we can only guess."

"It's possible," said Jane. "It's also possible your father was upset by something else. A letter or telegram, perhaps."

Helen turned to the door.

"Craven, you can come out."

The door opened and Craven appeared. He looked as nonchalant as ever.

"Yes, Miss Helen?"

"Did my father—"

"—receive any correspondence while you were away? No, Miss Helen. Neither did he send anything."

"Craven," said Kate. "Think hard. Are you able to say when his lordship's mood darkened?"

The butler thought for a moment.

"During Miss Helen's absence, his lordship was in and out of the house quite a bit. When he was here, he ate alone and he read a lot. It gave me time to get on with a few jobs of my own as well as some light reading. The few times I saw him, he was his usual civil self – which is to be expected. It would be most unseemly for a man in his position to discuss his concerns with a man in my position."

Helen turned to the amateur sleuths.

"Please don't let Miles know I've spoken to you. I just want the truth to come out."

"So do we," said Kate.

A few moments later, back in the car, Jane sighed.

"Where next?"

"I'm not sure," said Kate. "How about the school? I know the Roystons were incommunicado in Eastbourne at the time Herbert's mood soured, but there are one or two matters that still feel a bit off…"

Twenty-Five

It's often part of the design of truly grand houses that they're visible from some way off. The home of All Saints School for Boys was such a structure. Built as a private residence in 1868, and transformed into a school in 1888, it harked back to an earlier style with its simple, classical façade topped with a balustrade on the roofline.

Forty years after it became a school, Jane drove through the grand gates and past the old gatehouse, which was now home to the Headmaster and his wife.

A moment later, she brought the vehicle to a halt in the wide space available at the end of the drive. One other car was there, a dark blue Vauxhall 30–98 that looked to be five or so years old.

Kate got out and stretched her legs. Some way off, a dozen or more boys were running around on a rugby field, throwing and catching a ball. It really was the perfect day for outdoor sport.

"Did you know Herbert Longbottom's father?" asked Jane.

"Arthur? Yes, but only a little. When I told you about those long lunches? Herbert's father would stay in his rooms. He was getting on in years by the time I came on the scene and found it all a little tiring. Before that, he lived mainly in London. So, no – no strong memories of him."

"He had an influence on this place though."

"Yes, he did."

They headed for the main door, where Kate rang the bell. It didn't take long for it to be opened by a round-faced young woman with blonde hair tied in a bun.

"Hello, welcome to All Saints. How may I help?"

Kate beamed. "Good morning, or is it afternoon?"

"Afternoon. It's twenty past twelve."

"Right, well, I'm Mrs Forbes and this is Lady Jane Scott. We'd like to speak with Mr Royston, please."

"Are you thinking of sending a son here?"

This was aimed at Jane, who baulked a little.

"No," she said, "it's in connection with the murder of Lord Herbert Longbottom."

The young woman gulped. "Please do come in. I'm Miss Evans, the office junior clerk. Well, the only clerk. I work under Mrs Royston."

They followed Miss Evans through a grand vestibule that boasted a fabulous crystal chandelier, a stone fireplace, flower and nature themed oil paintings on the walls, and ornate plaster mouldings on the high ceiling. From there they entered a short corridor which led to a large, plain, modern space. On one side, behind a half-glass partition, was an office with two small desks, both with typewriters, and three metal filing cabinets. Kate and Jane, however, were asked to take a seat in a waiting area by a door marked 'Private'. Miss Evans knocked on this door and entered.

Kate took a seat, although Jane chose to remain standing.

A moment later, Miss Evans came back with a smile.

"Mr Royston won't be a moment."

She made for the office, although Jane was quick to engage her.

"You have quite modern office conditions."

"Yes, it's quite new – I mean compared with the rest of the building."

"Because of the fire?" asked Jane.

"Yes, that's right."

"How did that come about?"

"Oh… well… it was before my time, but it was a cigarette fire. Delia Trent was the clerical assistant at the time. A lovely lady who wouldn't harm a fly. Thankfully, she managed to get a job at the hospital. I mean, honestly, the way the newspapers reported it, you'd think the whole school burned down."

The door marked 'Private' swung open to reveal Guy Royston.

"Mrs Forbes, Lady Jane! Come in."

"Thank you, Headmaster," said Kate. "We're not disturbing your duties, I hope?"

"No, no, it's almost lunchtime."

They entered a huge plush study with more nature themed paintings, any number of ornaments, a Persian rug, a great oak desk, and two large bookcases packed full of academic-looking tomes.

"Please, take a seat."

They did so on the visitor side of the desk while Guy Royston went around to the other side and plonked himself down on a cushioned leather chair.

"Now… how can I help?"

"We just have a few questions, if that's alright?"

"Yes, of course."

"Mrs Forbes! Lady Jane! How's your investigation going?" It was Mrs Royston. She'd entered unseen and unheard through a side door.

"Mrs Royston, good afternoon," said Kate. "You'll be pleased to know we've made great strides. In fact, thanks to Lady Jane, there's been something of a turn in the tide."

"That sounds exciting."

"It is. The police are no longer certain of Robert Patterson's guilt."

"Really?" said the headmaster. "I thought they had him in custody."

"They do. It's just that with Jane's detective work upending the cart, they're now looking into other possibilities."

"I see… so poor Mr Patterson may yet be saved."

"That's our hope."

"Well," said Mrs Royston, "you did mention previously that the police can sometimes point their finger in the wrong direction. May I ask what Lady Jane discovered?"

"We can't say just yet," said Jane. "The police are keen to unsettle the real killer."

"Yes, of course."

"Lord Longbottom…" mused Kate. "Something serious was troubling him in the days before his death. You spoke with him at the town hall. Are you sure he never touched on the matter in question?"

"No, he didn't," said Guy Royston. "As I told you before, we had a brief chat about paintings."

"Yes, I was there and heard a little of it… as I was passing by, you understand. I'm certainly no snoop. That said, I recall you discussing *a* painting. That is, a single item. Are you able to tell us more?"

Guy shrugged. "No, sorry. I think he'd seen a good painting somewhere. Beyond that though…"

"Lord Longbottom was a friendly chap," said Kate. "He often attended social events. Here, that would be the school fete, prize-giving, sports day and so on. The thing is, his diary says he was due here on Monday at nine in the morning. Can you say why?"

"Yes, it was to discuss donating a suitable special prize for our fortieth anniversary prize-giving. Unfortunately, we'll never know what he had in mind."

"Perhaps it was the painting he mentioned," said Jane.

Guy nodded slowly.

"Yes, perhaps, although it's hardly a serious business. Speaking of it though has given me an idea. Miles Longbottom telephoned earlier. He wants us to go along to the hall tomorrow afternoon with thoughts on how to commemorate his father's life. An annual school prize in Lord Herbert Longbottom's name might be just the thing."

"That's wonderful," said Jane.

"The Longbottoms are part of the school's history," said Mrs Royston. "Miles and Ian are old boys; their grandfather was a trustee."

Kate smiled. This was getting them nowhere.

"Well, we'll trouble you no further," she said.

"Thanks for your time," added Jane.

"Not at all," said Guy. "Happy to help."

He got up and went to the door that led to the office and the exit.

"Miss Evans?" he called.

Miss Evans appeared in double-quick time.

"Headmaster?"

"Show our visitors out, would you?"

Miss Evans smiled and indicated the way. They exited and the door closed behind them.

"There's no need to take us to the front door," said Kate.

"It's no trouble at all," said Miss Evans. "I was only doing some filing."

"Do you enjoy working here?" asked Jane as they reached the grand vestibule.

"Yes, it's a smashing place to work. Some say it's haunted by a gardener from the previous house that stood here. I don't believe it though… although I probably wouldn't walk around the garden at night."

Arriving at the front door, she bade Kate and Jane farewell.

"Did that answer your questions, Aunt?" said Jane as they headed for the car.

Kate puffed out her cheeks.

"Jane… I have no idea."

"How about a visit to Fred Brigstock then? There are certainly some unanswered questions there."

"Agreed – but let's have some lunch first. Then we'll go and badger Mr Brigstock."

Twenty-Six

Following a quick cheese sandwich at Kate's house, they were soon back on the road and heading for the Brigstock farm.

"Will you always live in London?" wondered Kate as they cruised along a curving country lane.

"Possibly," said Jane.

"It's none of my business, but you're sure to live a long and happy life. I just wondered where."

"London, then, possibly."

"Northampton is a lovely part of the world," said Kate, mentioning the location of the Scott family seat.

"Yes, although London is so convenient."

"Yes, it is. I can see that."

Reaching a crossroads, they turned right.

"Brighton isn't a bad compromise," said Kate. "It's hardly London but it has more to offer than Sandham."

"Yes, I know it well from my schooldays."

Jane had attended the Roedean Girls' School just outside Brighton.

"It would suit you, Jane."

"Are you thinking of a hypothetical me?"

"I don't know. Am I?"

"A hypothetical me who's married with three adorable children…?"

"Sorry, Jane. I often see your future in that way. I think it's a disorder I have."

Jane smiled. "Perhaps one day."

The thought stirred Kate's spirits. "Right… well… Fred the farmer then. We'll have to explain that a box of veg isn't enough to buy us off."

"What if they offer us free eggs for life?"

"I think we should pray we're not tested that harshly, Jane."

A short while later, Jane once again brought the Triumph to a stop at the farmhouse gate. From there, they walked down the dried mud track to the farmhouse, giving thanks again for the continuing dry weather.

Halfway there, they stopped for a moment to talk to a goat, who was busy munching on some bramble.

"Hello there," said Kate. "I don't suppose you know if your owner was involved in the unfortunate death of Lord Longbottom?"

The goat carried on chewing.

"No? Fat lot of use you are then."

Jane laughed.

"Why don't we ask the man himself."

"Yes, we could also ask the man himself if we might borrow his goat. I've got brambles coming in from over the back at home. I mean once I've picked the blackberries, they're a nuisance."

"What are you really thinking, Aunt?"

"I'm thinking we know nothing about the Brigstocks. I'm also thinking that the police can't come at them from a friendly angle, but we can."

A moment later, they arrived at the ramshackle farmhouse, where Kate rapped on the door. Right away, they heard movement inside, and possibly a muttered curse. When Mrs Brigstock answered, she looked far from happy to see them.

"Mrs Brigstock," enthused Kate. "We're sorry to trouble you again. We townies sometimes have no idea how hard farm people work."

"Ain't that the truth!"

"Is your husband here?"

"He's at the cow shed, mucking out."

"Right, good," said Kate. "Oh, it's a lovely farm, but I can imagine it's not quite so lovely in frost-bound January or during endless rain in March."

"That's true enough."

"Farm folk are the backbone of Britain. That's what I always say – don't I, Jane?"

"You do, Aunt."

"The other thing I always say is that we'd all be in a right mess without the wonderful hard-working people who toil on the land."

"Well now… that's a fair observation, Mrs Forbes. It's not everyone who sees it like that."

"Perhaps they don't see you in town enough, so they aren't able to get a true picture."

"I'm not one for being out and about much. All that getting ready. I only go out if there's a need."

"Have you lived here all your life?" asked Jane.

"No, only since I married my Fred. The farm came down his family line. Gentlemen farmers, they were. His grandpop was the Honourable Richard Brigstock. But things were hard. Have you heard of the farming depression of late last century?"

"Yes," said Jane. "A terrible thing."

Kate knew of it too. The opening up of the American prairies led to sharp falls in worldwide grain prices, while the emergence of the steamship meant cheap and reliable transportation.

"Well," continued Mrs Brigstock, "Richard Brigstock rode it out by selling land to the Longbottoms. Nowadays, we're just ordinary farmers. We own most of what we farm, mind. That's something."

"It certainly is, Mrs Brigstock. May your livestock and crops flourish."

"Oh… bless you."

"We'll call on Fred, if that's alright."

"Yes, it's alright. It's just up the track there. Tell him I sent you."

They set off in silence, until they were out of earshot.

"Things haven't improved much for farmers since the Honourable Richard Brigstock's days," said Jane.

"No, indeed," said Kate.

A few minutes later, they entered the cow shed.

"Come to give me a hand, have you?" muttered Fred Brigstock. He was sweeping out manure from a stall.

Kate took a measured sniff.

"No, we've come to ask you about the Ridgeway housebuilding scheme."

"What about it?"

"Could we step outside?"

Fred tutted and led them out.

"What's all this about?" he demanded.

Kate took a breath of fresh air.

"What really made you change your mind?"

"You're not still banging on about Townsend, are you? I've already explained all that."

"Are you covering up for someone?"

"No, I'm not. I don't know why you'd think that."

"You're in league with Desmond Ainsley. He can be very persuasive."

"There's no cover up here."

"Are you sure? Lord Longbottom came to see you. What did he say?"

"I already told you. He was interested in what was going on, so I explained the scheme to him. It was more friendly than businesslike. That's how he was. A friendly man at heart who took an interest in Sandham's development. Now, if you don't intend to help, I'd best be getting on."

Jane smiled. "Mr Brigstock, I understand your family and the Longbottoms go back a long way."

"So?"

"I also understand that the Longbottoms extended their estate when they purchased land from your grandfather."

Fred seemed puzzled that they should know all this.

"Ancient history," he said.

"And yet, the Longbottoms don't farm. Whereas you do, as far as the eye can see."

"The Longbottoms own part of the land I farm. Not the best land, to be fair, so I only pay them a small rent for that bit. My grandpop wasn't stupid."

"Your family were once gentlemen farmers – the kind who don't get their hands dirty."

"Times change. I do have the choice of starving to death, of course."

Kate beheld the well-fed, pot-bellied farmer and wondered – but Jane continued calmly.

"I expect the Ridgeway scheme might help you there," she said. "Is any of that on Longbottom land?"

"None of it, no. Nor does it need Longbottom land to be connected to anything – roads, water, the railway…"

"So, no grudges or misunderstanding between you and Lord Longbottom then."

"No, none whatsoever. I'm even thinking we could name the new road up to the houses in a respectful way. Herbert Longbottom Drive or something."

"Has Miles invited you to the hall to discuss it?"

"How did you know that?"

Jane sidestepped it. "Just one other thing. Farmers all over the country are having a hard time of it. Many will resort to extra loans and overdrafts to get from one year to the next if their bank is friendly enough. Otherwise…"

"That's none of your business!"

"You're right, it's not. Can I just ask who you bank with, then we'll be gone."

Fred looked set to get angry, but it came out as a resigned sigh.

"Southern Counties."

"Ah, then you deal with the helpful Mr Swithin."

"I'm saying no more. Good day to you."

Jane and Kate bade him farewell and departed.

Back in the car, Jane started the engine.

"Now what?" said Kate.

"I'm not sure. Knowing that Desmond Ainsley is a money lender though…"

"He must be our killer, Jane. If there's any justice."

"If in doubt, Aunt, let's not lose sight of the one thing we can be certain of. Lord Longbottom was seriously troubled by something."

Kate thought for a moment.

"Alright, what if it was trouble with the school?"

"How do you mean?"

"What if Herbert suspected something was wrong? Financial mismanagement, for example. That might explain the fire."

"You mean a quick way to destroy inconvenient records five years ago?"

"Yes, exactly."

"Why not just toss them in a fireplace?"

"Well… yes, perhaps setting the building alight is a bit of a stretch."

"It wouldn't hurt to ask the person responsible about it though. Just to be sure. If I recall correctly, Delia Trent works at the hospital."

"Right, we'll leave the car at my place, Jane. It's only a few hundred yards and a healthy walk will boost our chances of avoiding a return there for other reasons."

Twenty-Seven

In 1837, as a small dispensary opened on East Avenue, north of the High Street. Thirty-two years later, the dispensary moved across the street into a larger building and became the Sandham Infirmary and Dispensary. A final move came in 1898, when it moved to a new building with grounds at the northern end of East Avenue and adopted the name Sandham Hospital.

Thirty years after a grand opening ceremony at which Herbert, as the new Lord Longbottom, cut the ribbon, Kate and Jane walked in through the main gates and up the short curving drive to the double doors, one of which was open. Inside, they stepped up to the unmanned desk, which meant ringing the bell.

A moment later, a middle-aged woman wearing small, round glasses emerged from the office behind the reception area and smiled.

"Good afternoon?"

"Good afternoon," said Kate. "We've come to see Mrs Trent. I understand she works in the office."

The receptionist frowned.

"Sorry, there's no Mrs Trent in the office here."

"Oh… we assumed it was Sandham Hospital. She must work somewhere else."

"We have a cleaner called Mrs Trent."

"Delia Trent?"

"Yes, that's her. I think she's somewhere out the back."

"Er…?"

The receptionist pointed left.

"Down that corridor all the way to the end. There's a refectory."

"Thank you."

Aunt and niece headed down the corridor and soon came to the right place – a canteen area. A woman in an apron was mopping the floor.

"Delia Trent?" asked Kate.

Mrs Trent stopped what she was doing and looked up. She seemed uncertain.

"Yes?"

"The same Delia Trent who worked at All Saints School?"

Now she looked worried.

"Yes…?"

Kate introduced herself and her niece before getting to the point.

"We're looking into the death of our friend, Lord Longbottom."

"Yes, I heard about that. What a shocking business. It's a good job they got the killer."

"Yes… do you mind if I ask how long you worked at All Saints?"

"Three years. Why do you need to know?"

"There was a fire."

Mrs Trent's mood darkened considerably.

"It's not something I like to think about."

"Can you tell us anything about it?" asked Jane.

"Why?"

"It's just background information, but occasionally it can be important. We're currently trying to learn all we can about Lord Longbottom's connection to the school."

"I'm sure his two sons went there."

"Yes… yes, they did. But then we learned about the fire, and we'd like to rule it out of any inquiries."

"I can't talk about it. It gave me nightmares."

"I'm not surprised."

"For months after, I'd wake up in the middle of the night thinking I'd burned down all kinds of things. The school, the pub, the theatre, my house. Terrible, it was. I couldn't work either. The newspapers said I was a reckless woman, so no one wanted to give me a job."

Kate felt a pang of sympathy.

"But you found something here."

Mrs Trent nodded.

"Not in the office, obviously. I'm a good cleaner, mind. If I see anyone throw a cigarette down, I'm there in an instant to sweep it up. Are you two smokers?"

"Er, no, we're not."

"Good. You'll be pleased to know I gave up smoking after the incident. I haven't been tempted back to it once."

Jane smiled warmly.

"Do you think you could tell us what happened."

She seemed reluctant to say.

"It's alright," said Kate. "We're sorry to have troubled you. I must say, the hospital is very fortunate to have such a conscientious employee."

They were about to leave, but Mrs Trent let out a sigh.

"The boys were playing rugby against another school. Everyone went to watch."

"So, you were left alone?" prompted Kate.

"Yes, it was lovely and quiet, so I thought I'd have a nice cigarette by the open window. Anyway, I put it on the edge of the ashtray on the desk for a minute so I could put some papers on the headmaster's desk. It's just that… on the way back, I got chased by a flippin' wasp. Well, I shooed it down to the main door and let it out, but… I can be a bit of a dreamer sometimes, so I stood outside for a bit, listening to the birds singing in the trees. I could hear the shouts from the rugby field too. By then, a gust must have blown the cigarette off the edge of the ashtray and set fire to the papers on the desk."

"It must have been such a shock," said Kate.

"I couldn't believe it. Half the office was on fire. I panicked for a bit and then ran out and called for help. The Headmaster and a few boys came running and managed to put it out with buckets of water from the tap in the backroom toilet."

"It must have been awful."

"It was. I was asked to go back the next day, but I didn't dare. All that damage I caused. Walls, ceiling, furniture, records, invoices, receipts… I've not been back since."

"It's completely understandable," said Kate. "We won't take up any more of your time."

They thanked her and departed.

"I'm not sure that gets us anywhere," said Kate as they headed for the exit.

"I wonder how Chief Inspector Ridley's getting on?" said Jane, perhaps by way of a suggestion.

Twenty-Eight

Heading west along the High Street, the right turn before Cobb Lane was Garston Row, home to Sandham Police Station – a gift in the will of Mrs Hurst before the War. It was, in fact, an ordinary detached house that had been modified and extended to include two custody cells, one of which currently held Robert Patterson.

Entering its front parlour in the early evening, Kate and Jane expressed their interest in speaking with Chief Inspector Ridley.

The doughty Sergeant Jones and affable Constable Harris, son of Winnie at the tea rooms, both shrugged.

"He's out and about," said Harris.

"Running around on the say-so of you two," added Jones in a way that made Ridley sound a fool.

With the police station proving to be a wrong turn, Kate and Jane thanked the uniformed pair and headed for Kate's house. They arrived there to the sound of the telephone ringing.

Seizing the receiver, Kate almost asked, "Chief Inspector?", but the voice on the line belonged to Lady Davenport.

"Kate, any luck?"

Kate wasn't sure what to say – a delay that elicited a decisive move on Pru's part.

"It's just that Christopher says he has an idea that will crack the case wide open."

"I do!" yelled Christopher into the phone, no doubt deafening Pru as he did so.

"Um…" was all Kate could say. Yes, Sir Christopher had been a top civil servant, but his form regarding great ideas had never been much to write home about.

"What's the idea?" Kate finally asked.

"I've no idea," said Pru. "He won't tell me. He says he only wants to speak to you. Hang on, I'll pass you over… Kate wants to know what's what."

"Righto," said Sir Christopher, taking the phone. "Kate, are you there?"

"Yes, fire away."

"Right, well… I intend to let every suspect know I believe I've identified the killer."

Kate frowned.

"I don't quite follow you."

"It's perfectly straightforward. I'll write to everyone who was at the town hall. Each recipient will think they're the only one I've written to. That way, I can make sure no-one slips through the net."

"Then what?"

"Well... when I write to them, I'll ask to meet with them. I'll say that I believe they can help me because I believe they know the killer too. Logically, one of them will be the real killer and think I'm onto them."

"Then what?"

"Well, whoever turns up to meet me – we nab them."

Before Kate could respond, a distant Pru could be heard.

"I'm not having some mad killer knocking at my door!"

"Don't be daft, old thing. I'd arrange to meet them somewhere quiet."

"Is that wise?" said Kate.

"Good point," said Sir Christopher. "I'll take the police with me."

"What if a curious innocent shows up?" said Kate.

"Oh, I'm sure the police would be able to tell if they're innocent."

Tell that to Robert Patterson, thought Kate.

"Unfortunately, fishing requires bait," she said. "Alas, we don't have anything specific to mention that would spook the killer."

"We have the falsified invitation card."

Kate pondered it.

"If we let that particular cat out of bag by posting everyone a letter, we'll be giving away our only ace to a killer who will be under no pressure to step out of the shadows."

"Hmm... back to the drawing board then."

He sounded disappointed.

Just then, the front door knocker sounded.

"I must go," said Kate. "I'll keep you and Pru posted if there are any developments."

A moment later, in the gathering evening gloom, she addressed the door.

"Hello?"

"Only me," said a familiar voice. "I just got your message."

Chief Inspector Ridley soon joined them to discuss matters over a cup of tea.

"You've been speaking to quite a few people," he said.

"I'm not sure we got anywhere though," said Kate. "It would seem we're missing something."

"I'm inclined to agree. While I can't go into confidential matters, I can say more generally that I spoke to Miles Longbottom and his brother. I'm not sure what to make of them. Very secretive, if you ask me. I don't have enough evidence to take it further though."

"We're not sure about them either," said Kate. "Lord Longbottom was troubled by a serious matter. Miles and Ian seem to be involved in something. Desmond Ainsley suggested it might be gambling debts."

"Interesting. There might be something in it. Urgent gambling debts, a bruised cheek..."

"Can you investigate it?"

"I'll need more than a rumour. I mean where's this gambling taking place? If it's poker, for example, those clubs in London are full of lords, ambassadors, generals and prime ministers, while the lower-class establishments are rife with thugs and villains."

"Not easy," said Jane.

"Hmm, what to do…?" muttered Kate.

"I'll look into it in the morning," said Ridley. "Who else have you seen?"

"Guy Royston at All Saints School," said Kate. "He insists he had a high regard for Lord Longbottom."

"There was a fire there a few years ago," said Jane. "I can't make anything of it though."

"We went to see Mrs Trent," said Kate. "She worked for the school at the time. It was her cigarette that caused it."

"Serious fire, was it?" Ridley asked.

"It did cause extensive damage to the office," said Kate.

Ridley shrugged. "It wouldn't be the first case of someone setting a fire to burn incriminating evidence. It's just that…"

"An intelligent criminal would use the fireplace?" suggested Jane.

"Exactly so. They don't usually look to draw attention to themselves."

"Which isn't the case when you risk burning the building down."

"I'm not sure it's a way forward," said Ridley. "Unless this Mrs Trent stood to gain?"

Kate shook her head.

"Mrs Trent had nothing to gain. It's clear even now that her nerves were shot through by the event. She's no criminal."

"You mentioned Desmond Ainsley," said Ridley. "I spoke with him earlier. He's a slippery eel, that one. I couldn't decide if he was trying to help me or help himself to making a friend at Scotland Yard for future use."

"It'll be the latter," said Kate.

"I also went to see Simon Townsend. He seems alright. I mean I get no sense that he's up to anything. Unlike Fred Brigstock, who I also saw. He's definitely hiding something."

"We saw him too."

"Hmm…" Ridley frowned. "I'm not sure it's a good idea for you to follow my every footstep. Nor me yours."

"We can step down, if you wish," said Kate. "It's like you said though. We occasionally get some useful gossip."

Ridley sighed. "We'll continue as we are for now."

Jane folded her arms.

"I'm puzzled. That counterfeit invitation suggests preparation and planning. It's possible the killer hasn't made any mistakes. Apart from us spotting the invitation card, that is – and that doesn't actually get us anywhere."

There was a knock the door.

"I'm not expecting anyone," said Kate.

She went to the front window, which just about afforded a sideways view of anyone at the front door.

"It's Fred Brigstock," she whispered to the others.

"I spooked him earlier," said Ridley. "He might clam up if he sees me again."

"Hide in the pantry."

"That door there," said Jane, pointing the way.

A moment later, Kate went to the front door and called softly.

"Who is it?"

"I'm sorry to trouble you in the evening, Mrs Forbes. It's Mr Brigstock, I'd like a word, if I might."

"You are aware there's a killer out there somewhere?"

"I'm not afraid."

"No, I mean women living alone shouldn't invite strange men into their homes at such times. Or anytime, really."

"Oh, I see what you mean. I'll be happy to stay here then. The thing is, I had your friend Ridley call on me earlier."

It occurred to Kate that if Fred were the killer and made a lunge at her, she would have Jane and the Chief Inspector to assist her in nabbing him.

She opened the door.

"Come in, Mr Brigstock."

He did so but stopped in the hall, where he nodded to Jane, who was standing by the pantry door.

"I won't stop," said the farmer. "As I mentioned, Ridley called on me."

"That's to be expected," said Kate.

"The thing is… I fear Desmond Ainsley."

"Why?"

Fred looked decidedly uncomfortable about telling tales.

"If things go wrong for him, he'll throw me to the wolves. I'm not saying he's committed a crime in his dealings with me, but he's shady. I want you to know in case things take a bad turn. If Desmond Ainsley is found to be involved in murder, I know he'd implicate me to protect himself."

Kate was beginning to feel a little agitated.

"Why deal with him, Mr Brigstock?"

"I don't want this getting around, but I've had a few financial problems. The housebuilding is meant to set me right again."

"Why didn't Mr Townsend's proposal solve that problem for you?"

"Because I thought I could ride it out. But I couldn't. Then Ainsley came along."

"And you don't think he's entirely honest?"

"No, but I'm innocent. I just want you to know that, and please feel free to tell your friend from Scotland Yard."

Kate bade him farewell and watched him head down the lane towards the High Street. Closing the door, she looked to the pantry, where Ridley emerged eating a biscuit.

"Sorry, I found it in a jar."

"Were you able hear him?" asked Kate.

"Yes, but he's playing the same game as everyone else. They're all innocent and it's somebody's else's fault."

"What's the next move then?"

Ridley shrugged.

"Sorry, but unless any of us can come up with some concrete evidence, I have a man who was at the scene, potentially bore a grudge, and was found with the poison in his pocket."

Kate sighed. It wasn't looking good for Mrs Patterson's boy.

Twenty-Nine

After a dinner of steamed trout and buttery mashed potato followed by stewed apple, Kate and Jane were sitting comfortably in armchairs either side of the fireplace. With the night-time temperature dropping Kate had lit a small fire.

"How do you *really* feel about being an unofficial consulting detective, Jane?"

Kate's niece gave it some consideration before answering.

"On the verge of making a hash of it, Aunt."

"Who killed Herbert Longbottom?" mused Kate. "While he was talking to Mrs Deane about hanging baskets, he drank sherry. He then told her that the man she should ask was Sir Christopher – at which point the poison overwhelmed him. If Robert Patterson isn't our murderer, there's no shortage of those with the opportunity. As for the means… it's not impossible to slip a small, slim bottle into a man's jacket pocket. It's the motive though. That's the struggle."

Jane contemplated it.

"Robert Patterson swears he's moved on since Lord Longbottom brought his military career to a premature end, but revenge is a strong motive."

"Except Robert was set up with a forged invitation card."

"Yes, I still believe the real killer is using him to take the blame."

Kate nodded. "So, who is our hidden killer? Is it Miles Longbottom?"

"In terms of a motive – what if he's been selling off family heirlooms? It would explain why Lord Longbottom was studying the family inventory."

"It might also explain a bruised cheek. Although…"

"Yes, Aunt?"

"Herbert never had the opportunity to strike Miles."

"No, but Ian did."

"Ian? Yes… of course…"

"It's only a possibility," cautioned Jane. "There's no evidence of Miles selling things off."

"Hmm… those two do seem to be involved in something though. What if Herbert discovered their secret and decided to cut them off? As possibilities go, it's a strong one – even if we don't know what the secret is."

"Yes, it's possible. Of course, we shouldn't overlook Fred Brigstock and Desmond Ainsley."

"Yes, a shady deal… and one that would put Mr Ainsley in prison. That's surely motive enough, and not just because I think he's a pompous peacock."

"Fred Brigstock needed money," said Jane. "Farmers were encouraged to take on debt during the War to maximise production. Afterwards… lots of equipment, plenty of debt, and overproduction meaning falling prices. He could be more desperate than he's letting on."

"Yes… then there's Guy Royston, Jane. He's been acting oddly."

"Lord Longbottom wanted to see him on Monday morning. Was it to do with prizes for prize-giving? Or something else?"

Kate sighed. "Where are we going with this? For all we know, someone like Simon Townsend could be playing us all for fools. I mean we're assuming Herbert was in support of his scheme. What if he wasn't? What if Simon is the dubious one?"

"It would mean him being in cahoots with someone at the function, which unfortunately takes us all the way back to Robert Patterson."

"Yes, a joint enterprise. We can't rule it out. You know, I think some warm cocoa is needed."

Kate rose from her chair and went into the kitchen. Jane followed.

"I hope this doesn't wreck your lunch appointment tomorrow, Aunt."

"That's my hope too. We have a table booked for one o'clock."

Jane smiled. "I think it's bloomin' great. You two should have more lunches together. And dinners. And walks."

"I thought we'd agreed I wouldn't rush into it."

Kate took two cups and put a couple of teaspoons of cocoa powder into each.

"Uncle Henry is forever in our hearts, Aunt. We'll never forget him."

Kate relaxed a little.

"You've already told me he'd approve. We must go slowly though."

Jane puffed out her cheeks.

"Sorry for my impatience. I just want you to be happy, that's all."

Kate smiled. "I know you mean well."

She used a cloth to lift the kettle, which had been sitting on the end of the range since dinner. She then poured warm water into the cups and stirred.

"How about six months?" said Jane. "Do you know, I've never been a bridesmaid?"

"Hey, you can't make such pronouncements and be silent about your own situation."

"Touché, Aunt Kate. No, Harry and I aren't ready yet. And before you mention me being twenty-seven, I still feel young. Besides, we both have work we want to complete."

"But that's the thing, Jane. You both work in historical research. It will never be finished."

They took a cup each and returned to their seats by the fire.

"Jane… can I be honest?"

"Please."

"One day, you'll look up from your books and see a fiftieth birthday card with your name on it. Will that be a good time for marriage? And before you counter me, let me say that time really does fly. The years… I can't tell you how fast they slip by. Remember, I was your age once, so don't say I'm wrong."

Jane sipped her cocoa and thought for a moment.

"I told a fib."

"Oh?"

"Harry *is* ready."

"Ah. Do you think you love him?"

"I know I do."

Kate felt the warmth of the cup in her hands.

"Change can certainly derail us." She thought of life before and after Henry. "But it can also send us on exciting new journeys."

"I will marry him, Aunt Kate. I'll tell him soon enough."

"Six months? A year or two? Sorry, I'm teasing. It's what you've been telling me."

Jane laughed softly. "Perhaps we're hurtling towards a double wedding."

"Oh, I doubt that," said Kate, although the idea tickled her.

"Pru and Sir Christopher are a lovely couple," said Jane after a pause.

"Yes, they are… loyal and endearing… and occasionally surprising. Especially Christopher. I think the chief inspector found his chalkboards a little odd."

"Yes…"

"And as for Eric the engine… and the offer to trap the killer by sending a letter…" Kate stared into the glowing fire. "When Henry passed away, the first person to cheer me up was Pru. She left it just the right amount of time… you know, to allow me all those quiet evenings I needed. Then, on a glorious summer's day, she took me to lunch. Not to the Crown Hotel, but to a bench overlooking the sea. She arranged for Winnie at the tea rooms to send sandwiches and cold drinks… and Pru and I sat there for ages… and it was perfect."

Kate looked to her niece, but Jane appeared to have been struck by a thought.

"Jane? What is it?"

"Something you said. I can't think why it didn't occur to me before, but there it is."

"There *what* is?"

"Aunt, I suddenly feel we're a whole lot closer to the answer."

Thirty

On a sunny but chilly Saturday morning, Jane took it steady as she steered the Triumph off the main road into a quiet, leafy lane. As far as Kate was concerned, there was no hurry. The case was potentially a step closer to being solved.

She soon spotted the house up ahead on their left – a grey stone, two-storey, early Georgian pile.

"Here we are then…"

Jane drove through the gates onto the short drive. A moment later, she came to a halt by the garage – the doors of which were open, revealing the space to be empty.

"Right," said Kate. "We're unofficial investigators. Let's do our best."

As they got out of the car, Craven appeared at the hall's front door.

"Mrs Forbes, Lady Jane… Miss Helen said to show you directly to the sitting room."

They followed the trusty retainer through the vestibule and into a short corridor, where he opened the sitting room door for them.

Helen was standing by the window.

"Mrs Forbes, Lady Jane… Miles isn't here. Nor is Ian."

"Oh, we were hoping they might spare us a moment," said Kate.

"Chief Inspector Ridley was here earlier. He had a word with them."

"About what?"

"I wasn't in the room… but from what I could make out, he wanted to know where Miles worked."

"Oh?"

"Sorry, I didn't get much more than that."

"Do you know where your brothers went?"

"Yes, Brighton."

"Brighton?"

"Yes, Ian's moving into a new place there."

Kate was surprised. "Nobody mentioned Ian moving to Brighton."

"It's not important, is it?"

"Possibly not."

"They'll be back this afternoon for the meeting."

"Yes, of course."

"We need your help with something," said Jane. "The Longbottom inventory. We need to see it."

"Ah right… this way."

They followed Helen into a study opposite the sitting room. Craven followed as far as the door.

"We keep old stuff in here," said Helen, indicating a large rosewood cabinet.

She turned the handle – but without success.

"Miles must have locked it."

"Is that unusual?" asked Kate.

"I'm not in here much, but I don't recall it ever being locked."

Helen turned to Craven, who was no doubt awaiting orders to let him leave.

"Do we have a key for this cabinet?"

"That's um… difficult for me to answer, Miss Helen."

Kate smiled at him.

"Your loyalty to the head of the house is commendable. However, Lady Jane and I are tracking down the previous head of the household's cold-blooded murderer. Are you certain you want to be on the wrong side of justice?"

"No, but…"

"My brother isn't Lord Longbottom yet," said Helen. "At least not as per the usual etiquette." By this, she meant the protocol of not using a title until after the funeral of the previous incumbent.

"Yes, um…" uttered the dithering butler.

But Kate fixed him with a steely glare.

"Craven, a chance to nab the killer might be lost to us if you choose to just stand there."

"Yes, well… you might try the desk drawers. I think I may have seen Mr Miles in action thereabouts."

They soon had the key.

In a trice, the cabinet was open, and Helen was handing the Longbottom inventory to Kate. She, in turn, handed it to Jane.

Jane slowly ran a finger down the first page, squinting to read the entries.

"Quill and ink can be quite squiggly," said Helen, almost apologetically.

"It's fine," said Jane. "Your grandfather was quite a collector."

"Yes, he was. My father, not so much."

"There are so many items here." Jane turned the page, and then another. "Thirty, forty paintings… Aphrodite, Two Ladies in Venice, The Toils of Sisyphus, Revenge, Merlin's Wrath…" She squinted harder to read something more. "Some of the entries have additional notes…" She then looked up at Kate and Helen. "That's interesting. One of these paintings is on loan to P."

Kate frowned. "Who's P?"

Helen took the inventory but could only shrug.

"I've no idea. It looks like my grandfather's handwriting, only he died before I was born. Craven, I expect that's long before your time too?"

"Yes, Miss Helen."

"What about your predecessor?" asked Kate.

"No longer with us, madam."

"Are there any other staff from way back?"

Craven shook his head.

"The police want this resolved as soon as possible," sighed Kate. "Yet now we have another mystery on our hands."

"There's something we can check right away though," said Jane. "Come on, Aunt. Let's go."

Thirty-One

At Desmond Ainsley's front door, Kate rapped forcefully on the knocker.

"His car's not here. Perhaps he's out."

Kate knocked again.

"Do you know who Mr Ainsley reminds me of?" she whispered.

"No."

"Calvin Croft."

"Who?"

"Calvin Croft – a hideous, middle-aged chap we all tried to avoid when I was young. He'd be at every social event, smiling smarmily at the ladies. If you looked into his eyes, you could see an abacus totting up your worth. We called him Calculating Croft. He spent several years trying to hook the richest, most gullible woman he could find. In the end, he married Betty Edwards, the only offspring of an elderly wealthy man. A mean man too. He disliked Croft, so he kept the flow of funds strictly limited. In fact, such was the level of the old man's ire, he purposely lived to the age of ninety-two so that he could outlive Croft by one day. Betty then inherited the lot and married the local vicar."

Kate knocked again.

"It was in a back room, Aunt…"

"Yes, it was, wasn't it."

Aunt and niece moved nonchalantly to the corner of the house, and then swiftly down the side alley, where Jane climbed the five-foot wall and slid the gate bolt open to let her aunt in.

A moment later, they were at the study window, where they gained a clear view of a painting on an easel less than ten feet away.

"What do you see?" prompted Jane.

"Desmond Ainsley's latest acquisition."

"A painting, yes – of what?"

Kate shrugged. "A boat. Or to be precise, an old ship."

"Let's be even more precise. It's an English ship of the late-Tudor period. Apart from that, the background looks like a Tudor fort. Is it starting to make sense to you?"

"Er… not quite, Jane."

"Revenge, Aunt. Revenge."

"As in Robert Patterson exacting revenge on Herbert Longbottom?"

"No, think of the paintings in the Longbottom inventory. Merlin's Wrath… um, The Toils of Sisyphus,

Revenge… It's tempting to think of Revenge as a painting about an emotion. Some Biblical scene in the style of Michaelangelo, perhaps."

"Right," said Kate. "I'm going to take a wild guess. The name of the ship in Desmond Ainsley's painting is Revenge."

"Yes, Aunt. These days, all British warships bear the prefix HMS."

"His or Her Majesty's Ship."

"Yes, but that convention didn't come about until long after the Tudors. Hence, it's Revenge, not HMS Revenge."

"You knew as soon as you saw it in the inventory."

"I did. Despite Mr Ainsley's assault on our sensibilities in the study the other day, the painting registered somewhere at the back of my mind."

"Well, despite what I think of Desmond Ainsley, it's not a bad work of art."

"It's likely to be Revenge moored at Tilbury."

"Why so?"

"It's where Queen Elizabeth inspired her fleet to take on the Spanish Armada. I expect you know her famous speech."

"Um…?"

"From a distant memory of my studies, it starts along the lines of… 'I know I have the body of a weak and feeble woman, but I have the heart and stomach of a king, and of a king of England too, and think foul scorn that Parma or Spain, or any prince of Europe, should dare to invade the borders of my realm.' She knew exactly how to rouse the hard-boiled sea captains of the time. Revenge was in Sir Francis Drake's fleet which raided Cadiz in 1587 and also part of the fleet that defeated the Spanish Armada the following year."

"It's fascinating history, Jane – and you will certainly one day be a professor of the subject at Oxford… but how does it fit into our understanding of who killed Herbert Longbottom?"

"Forgive me, Aunt, but I need to go through a number of possible permutations. I'd hate to jump to a wrong conclusion."

The sound of feet on gravel caught their attention.

"Ainsley?" wondered Kate.

They went round to the front, where a middle-aged woman was just going in. She was clutching a small paper bag with great care.

"Oh!" she gasped on spying them. "If you've been knocking, I nipped out for eggs. How can I help?"

"We were hoping to speak with Mr Ainsley," said Kate.

The woman frowned.

"It wouldn't be Mrs Forbes and Lady Jane, would it?"

"Yes, that's right."

"Oh… dear me. I'm Mrs Hibbert, the housekeeper. Mr Ainsley left a message in case you called."

Kate liked efficiency. "What was it?"

"Well, I'm only the messenger but he said to clear off and not come back."

"He's lost none of his charm, has he," said Kate.

"He can be a bit rude," agreed Mrs Hibbert. "All I can tell you is he won't be back from Brighton 'til this afternoon. He has a meeting of some sort at Longbottom Hall."

"But right now, he's in Brighton?"

"Yes, he has a property there."

Kate sighed and checked her watch.

"We ought to be collecting someone soon, Jane."

"Yes, the professor. Before we do though, I need to make an urgent call." She turned to the housekeeper. "Would you mind if I used Mr Ainsley's telephone to speak to the police?"

"Er… I suppose it's alright if it's the police. It's at the end of the hall."

"It's also confidential," said Jane going in and pushing the door to.

Kate smiled at Mrs Hibbert and pointed to the shrubs on the other side of the driveway. "They're doing well. Does Mr Ainsely have a gardener. Only I don't see him as the green-fingered type."

"Yes, he has a gardener. If you must know, it's a chap call Bennett…"

Kate worked hard on the small talk for the next few minutes with a wholly uninterested and suspicious audience. She was glad when Jane emerged from the house.

"Right, let's go, Aunt."

They thanked Mrs Hibbert and returned to the Triumph.

"What did the police have to say?" asked Kate.

"The police?"

"You just telephoned them."

"No, I called the Grosvenor Gallery in Brighton. I wanted to know if Desmond Ainsley bought that painting from them as he claims."

"And did he?"

"The proprietor refused to say."

"You should have mentioned Scotland Yard."

"I did, but he said let them come. Apparently, his books are squeaky clean, and he has nothing to hide."

"I see."

Jane started the car.

"Aunt, your country cottage painting…?"

"What about it?"

"Do you mind if we sell it at half its value?"

"Why would we do that?"

"To catch a killer, of course."

Thirty-Two

At a quarter past eleven, Jane brought the Triumph to a halt outside Sandham Station. There were two other cars parked outside, while half a dozen passengers had just disembarked from a train on the opposite platform to the one Perry Nash's train would pull into.

"Perfect," said Kate. "Five minutes to spare. We can sit quietly and replenish our reserves."

"It poses a problem though, Aunt Kate. A rather serious one."

"Oh?"

"Well, this is a four-seater."

"Yes," said Kate, admiring Jane's trusty Triumph.

"Yes, so think about the seat configuration."

"Pardon?"

"Well, if you and I sit in the front, neither of us will be able to make the professor feel welcome."

"Oh…"

"Perhaps you should sit alongside him in the back."

"No, Jane, then you'd look like our chauffeur."

"Yes, but crucially I wouldn't be able to see what you two were getting up to."

"Jane, really! I'm quite certain we wouldn't be getting up to anything. However, now you've raised it, Perry will be just fine in the back. I'm perfectly capable of lobbing the odd *bon mot* over my shoulder."

"If you say so, Aunt. That's the diplomacy problem tackled then."

A few minutes later, over the picket fence, a train came in accompanied by the shriek of brakes on metal wheels. This was quickly followed by three people leaving the station building. While two of them strode purposefully off, the other, a grey-haired chap in his fifties holding a small travel bag, stood by the entrance looking uncertain, as if he'd got off at the wrong stop.

"There he is," said Jane.

When Kate first met Professor Peregrine Nash at Penford, her first thoughts were that he was intelligent, pleasant, handsome, and a widower… not that she'd been interested in that sort of thing.

That, of course, had changed. It wasn't the big things that did it. It was the small things, like the occasion they both wore Panama hats and each picked up the wrong one, so that Perry's sat high on the top of his head like a comic prop, while hers fell straight down to her eyebrows. Jane cheekily suggested they should write their names in them.

It was a funny moment – but for Kate it was also a moment of connection, of being one of two.

She got out of the car and called out.

"Perry, over here."

He turned and realised that the Austin he was expecting to see had been replaced by a Triumph. His smile was one of warmth and confusion.

"Kate… Jane…?"

He came over to the car.

"Um…?"

"Hello, Professor," said Jane.

"The thing is, Perry," said Kate, somewhat hesitantly, "there's been a murder."

"Ah yes, Lord Longbottom. I read about it in the *Daily Telegraph*. You're not involved, are you?"

Kate thought how to best frame her response.

"To a degree."

"Up to our eyebrows," countered Jane.

"Oh dear," sighed Perry.

"It's alright," said Kate. "Jane and I are acting with the approval of Chief Inspector Ridley of Scotland Yard. It also looks like Jane might be on the point of cracking the case."

"I see," said Perry. "So, what's happening with lunch?"

Jane smiled.

"There's been a change of plan."

"Oh?"

"Yes, hop in the back," said Kate. "We're going to Brighton."

"Brighton?"

"Yes, we'll definitely have lunch at some point, but before we do, we might need your help in a little subterfuge."

"Really?"

"What do you know about art?" asked Jane.

"Um…?"

"Don't worry," said Kate. "We'll get you up to speed on the way."

Thirty-Three

Kate was grateful for the fine October weather. Having Jane drive them along the coastal byways in glorious sunshine made it feel like the South of France. Not that she had ever been there.

Passing through seaside Hove, the view of Brighton's West Pier up ahead to their right made Kate think of stopping. Not to enjoy an out of season ice-cream but to learn more about the fortunes of the pier. These marvels of engineering were mostly for those seaside towns that lacked a harbour. Sandham Harbour of course provided plenty of shelter and excellent landing places, hence no need for a Sandham Pier. But now? In the modern era? Wasn't a pier an attraction in itself?

Reaching Brighton, they turned away from the sea and headed into the heart of the town. With Saturday lunchtime almost upon them, there were lots of people out shopping.

It wasn't long before they pulled over opposite a row of smart shops in the busiest part of the town. One of these was the Grosvenor Gallery.

"Right," said Jane. "Now we wait."

"Wait for what?" said Perry.

Jane pointed. "It looks like the proprietor has a couple of customers. Possibly, a husband and wife. Let's wait until we have him alone."

It occurred to Kate that such an establishment would operate on selling the occasional expensive painting to the occasional wealthy customer. It wasn't like the baker's in Sandham High Street with its morning queues.

A few minutes later, the couple left the shop empty-handed.

Jane went in first. She had Kate's countryside cottage painting under her arm.

"Right," said Kate, turning to face Perry on the back seat. "We'll give her a minute or two."

"Yes, right," he replied, sounding very much ill-at-ease with a murder inquiry.

Despite the impending crick in her neck, Kate maintained her posture as a courtesy to her friend.

"With a bit of luck, Perry, we'll be able to make progress before the Chief Constable's pressure forces the issue in the wrong direction."

"The Chief Constable… yes."

Kate felt a sympathetic pang. The poor chap had come for lunch. Only, she wasn't sure what to discuss in such a short interval. Idle chit-chat was always harder than it seemed. Then again, an interesting discussion might delay their gallery plan, especially if Perry warmed to the subject. And as for discussing their future…

"Chief Constable!" she exclaimed.

"Pardon?"

"I wonder why he's called that?"

"Why whose called what?"

"Why the Chief Constable's called the Chief Constable."

"Oh… because it's the most senior police role in the county."

"Why not call himself the Big Boss then?"

Perry laughed. "Perhaps he does."

Kate laughed too and felt more relaxed.

"His name's Sir Ronald Hope," she said. "Some call him Sir Ronald Hopeless."

"Tsk, Kate."

As it was, they fell silent. Kate wanted to squeeze his hand and say it was lovely to see him, but they were sitting in a motorcar waiting to fool an art dealer.

"It's quite an interesting piece of history," said Perry after fifteen long seconds.

Kate smiled, which he took as license to continue.

"It's not my period at all – far too recent – but the earlier history is there." He was sitting forward now. "As I understand it, the term 'Constable' dates back two or three centuries to the original parish constables, when policing was informal. When the whole business was formalised during the last century, the link to the past was kept. I think the idea was to show it was long-established and therefore nothing to fear."

"Fear?" queried Kate.

"Yes, fear. In the early 19th century, many were concerned that the introduction of a modern police force might in practice be a government paramilitary force created solely for the purposes of control."

"I see. Thankfully, that never happened."

"Indeed," said Perry, "but it explains why the most senior police office in the county is called the Chief Constable, and that he is aided by those with non-military titles, such as superintendents and inspectors. In fact, it's only the sergeant, one rank above the lowly, ordinary constable, who bears a military title."

"How fascinating."

"I believe the word 'Constable' comes from the Latin, *stabuli*, which means a keeper of the stables. He would have been a respected figure at a strictly local level. Ultimately, it was use of a historical link to reassure people."

"Well," said Kate, "whether its policing of centuries past or today, there are villains who walk among us, and who must be caught."

"Yes, indeed," said Perry. "I assume that means it's time to act."

"Precisely."

Thirty-Four

By the time Kate and Perry entered the Grosvenor Gallery, a price for the countryside cottage painting had seemingly been agreed, because Jane was giving her details for the proprietor to log in his book. She was then required to sign a document stating she was the rightful owner.

"It's just that I'm occasionally offered stolen items," he explained.

Some cash was then handed over.

"Thanks. I'll just have a browse," said Jane.

The proprietor smiled and turned his attention to his other recent arrivals.

"Welcome to the Grosvenor Gallery. Oswald King, proprietor, at your service."

"Hello, I'm Professor Peregrine Nash and this is my wife, Mrs… er…"

"Nash…?" guessed the proprietor.

"Quite so."

Mrs Nash? Kate felt her face flush.

"Is there anything specific you're interested in?" asked Mr King.

"Yes," said Perry, "we've come to look at paintings that feature…"

It took the professor a full second to decide, in which time Kate thought it wise to step in. Hence Perry's choice of paintings featuring 'horses' trailing Kate's choice of 'fish' by a fraction of a second – thus giving the impression of a joint interest in "Fi-shorses."

This was rapidly followed by "Fish!" and "Horses!"

"Um…" Oswald King seemed perplexed.

"Are there any with both?" asked Kate.

"No, madam," said the bemused dealer. "It's not a common combination of subjects."

"Either will do," said Perry.

"Ooh," proclaimed Kate, spotting a very large oil on canvas tableau of a group of clergymen outside an ancient Greek building. The price tag was £45. "Just what I'm looking for."

Out of the corner of her eye, she spotted Jane slipping in behind the counter.

"It's not a Rembrandt, is it?"

"Er, no, madam, but look at the way the artist has captured the light. It's certainly reminiscent of Rembrandt's style, and at a very fair price."

Somewhat alarmingly for the proprietor, Kate removed the oversized painting from the wall and wobbled into the better light by the window. The terrified owner failed to notice Jane checking his record book.

"Madam, will you please put that painting down."

"I thought you said it would capture the light."

"No, the artist has already done that for you. No additional light is required to enjoy the work."

"It's quite heavy, isn't it. Perry…?"

Perry took hold of one side.

"Are we taking it outside?" he asked.

"No, you are *not* taking it outside! Not unless you intend to buy it."

"Buy it?" gasped Perry. "Can't see a blessed horse in it anywhere. Unless it's hiding behind that pillar."

"We should buy it," said Kate. "It's rare to get a Rembrandt for forty pounds."

"It's not a Rembrandt!" protested the proprietor. "I never claimed it was! And the price is forty-*five* pounds!"

"Did you hear that, Perry. He's added another fiver on for a mere copy of a Rembrandt."

Again, she caught sight of Jane – this time waving as she emerged from behind the counter.

"I've changed my mind," said Kate. "I think I'll buy a potted Ficus instead."

"Are you ready?" said Jane, seemingly joining them from out of thin air.

Perry Nash nodded. "Yes… um… Guinevere… my daughter. Let's go."

They departed hastily and got back into the car. From across the street, the proprietor glared at them from his doorway.

"Any luck?" asked Kate.

"Yes," said Jane. "Desmond Ainsley did indeed buy Revenge from the Grosvenor Gallery. It's in the transactions book."

"He didn't steal it then?" said Kate, sounding disappointed.

"No, but the main point was to learn who the gallery acquired it from."

"And…?"

"Mr Jenkins, 72, Milburn Place, Brighton. The gallery bought two paintings from him six months ago."

"What are you thinking?" asked Kate.

"I'm thinking… Venus."

"Venus?"

"Who *is* Mr Jenkins?" asked Perry.

"A mystery," said Jane. "Of course, he could be an innocent art dealer who acquired Revenge from P."

"P…?" said Perry.

"Let's see if Mr Jenkins can help us," said Kate. "Oh, to think Ginny has missed all this excitement."

"Who's Ginny?" said Perry.

"A friend we had lunch with on Wednesday, which feels like a lifetime ago!"

It didn't take long to find a policeman and ask for directions to Milburn Place – which turned out to be on the eastern edge of Brighton, away from the busy centre.

"Just to be clear," said Perry as they reached the beginning of the street in question, "who exactly are we expecting to answer the door?"

"I've a feeling I won't be surprised," said Kate.

With Milburn Place having its odd and even numbers on either side, it was a simple matter of reaching the higher numbers and slowing as they passed 66, 68, 70…

"Oh," said Kate. "That's a surprise!"

"On the contrary," said Jane. "It makes perfect sense."

"Why would Mr Jenkins give an address that doesn't exist?" questioned Perry.

Kate sighed. "Because Mr Jenkins doesn't exist either."

Now Perry frowned. "Are you really working with Scotland Yard?"

"Only as eyes and ears. Especially ears. Of course, he'd be delighted if we came up with some actual evidence."

"What's your next move then?"

"Unless we can work out who P is, there might not be a next move."

"Don't fret, Aunt," said Jane. "I worked out who P is ten minutes ago."

"Oh!" said Perry. "So, there *is* to be a next move then?"

"Yes, three of them," said Jane. "First, we need to find a telephone and make a call to Chief Inspector Ridley…"

"And the second?" asked Kate.

"We need to call in at Brigstock Farm."

"To see Mr Brigstock?"

"No, to see his wife. If we're very respectful and promise that what she tells us will land Desmond Ainsley in it up to his neck, I think she'll come through."

"Right."

"You mentioned a third move," said Perry.

"Ah yes! We have a meeting to gatecrash!"

Thirty-Five

Kate, Jane and Perry Nash arrived in Jane's Triumph at the gates of Longbottom Hall at around a quarter to three. A police car waiting opposite contained Chief Inspector Ridley, Sergeant Jones and two others. Constables Harris and Edmonds were beside it on bicycles.

Right away, the two motor vehicles proceeded up to the house where they parked alongside several other cars – among which Kate recognised the Longbottoms' Rolls-Royce Silver Ghost, Desmond Ainsley's Rolls-Royce Phantom and the Davenports' somewhat more modest Alvis Tourer.

"Just in time for tea and cake," she said somewhat hopefully. There was always a chance that the business of murder could knock refreshments off the agenda.

A few moments later, Craven showed them to the ground floor's main room – a grand salon that was twice the size of the sitting room, and boasted twice the number of fireplaces, chandeliers and paintings. Kate remembered it from those far-off days of convivial lunches that would spill out onto the lawn in summertime.

They only caught a small snippet of proceedings: Mr Swithin saying how the family could rely on his bank during the transition period – which Kate took to mean an overdraft if needed while death duties drained their account.

Then, without exception, all eyes turned to the new arrivals, who appeared to have stormed rudely into an innocuous chat about ideas to commemorate the life of Lord Herbert Longbottom.

From her place among the standing incomers, Kate beheld those seated around the room:

Mr Swithin.

Pru and Sir Christopher.

The Reverend Piers Drysdale and his wife, Dorothy.

The Headmaster of All Saints School, Guy Royston and his wife, Hilda.

Desmond Ainsley and Fred Brigstock.

Ian and Helen Longbottom… and, last but certainly not least, their brother, Miles, who seemed uncertain who to address first.

"Chief Inspector?" he eventually uttered.

"Here to pay your respects?" added Ian Longbottom.

"Yes and no," said Ridley. "Until a short while ago, I believed that Lord Herbert Longbottom spoke with his killer sometime on Friday or Saturday last."

"You no longer do?" asked Miles.

"Correct. To be clear, that's when his lordship's mood darkened considerably. We know this from Miss Helen Longbottom, who left him on Friday in good spirits but found him troubled when she returned on Sunday morning to attend church with him."

"He wouldn't confide in me," said Helen.

Ridley nodded. "Thanks to Mrs Forbes, we also know that Lord Longbottom planned to discuss his concern with the relevant person at the town hall on Wednesday evening in his preferred manner – which was to have a quiet word."

Kate confirmed it.

"I spoke with Herbert on the promenade after lunch on Wednesday. He was hoping to resolve the matter that evening."

"I'm sorry to interrupt," said Fred Brigstock, "but I was there on Wednesday, and I saw with my own eyes how that Patterson bloke had the poison on him. Since then, I've heard there's a doubt."

"Yes," said Miles. "I have to say we're all in the dark."

Again, Ridley nodded. "Yes, it was quickly established that Patterson was the killer. He had the poison in his pocket, and he seemingly had a motive regarding a long-held grudge. However, some doubt was cast on Patterson's guilt by Lady Jane Scott."

"Yes, but what doubt?" demanded Ian Longbottom.

"We'll come to that in a minute," said Ridley.

"I still say it's Patterson," said Mr Swithin.

Ridley ignored him. "We know Lord Longbottom was looking into a number of matters. We also know he was killed to silence him. The question has always been who was he planning to have a quiet word with on Wednesday evening regarding a troublesome matter? Because that's the person who brought cyanide to the town hall in order to commit murder."

"Really," huffed Ian. "If it wasn't Robert Patterson, then who!"

"I've had some assistance with this from Mrs Forbes and Lady Jane Scott," said Ridley. "I think it's time for one of them to throw a little light on proceedings."

Kate immediately took a step back. Over the past three cases, this had proven to be Jane's speciality. Her niece still looked to her for permission though.

Kate gave a little nod, leaving Jane to turn to face the gathering.

"There's a murderer among us," she said. "A week ago, Lord Longbottom learned of certain goings on regarding the Ridgeway housebuilding scheme. Last Friday he went to see Simon Townsend. The day after that, he came to see you, Mr Brigstock."

Fred Brigstock tensed up. "I told him it was just a change of mind… and that Mr Ainsley had offered me a better deal."

Jane turned to Desmond Ainsley.

"Lord Longbottom then came to see you, Mr Ainsley. You and he had a chat in your study."

"Yes, we did – and he left satisfied that everything was above board."

"Above board? He'd learned from Simon Townsend that Fred Brigstock had a serious debt problem. Simon had been pleasant and respectful to Fred's wife, which is a good way to learn a thing or two. The good news was a demand for new homes – and a chance for you, Mr Brigstock, to make some money by letting Mr Townsend develop the best plot."

Fred said nothing but glanced grimly at Ainsley.

"Ah," said Jane, "but then Desmond Ainsley got wind of it. We spoke with Mrs Brigstock on the way here. People with money problems will often use private lenders at extortionate rates when they've been turned away by Mr Swithin. We know you owed money to a lender."

"Not Mr Ainsley?" groaned the vicar, although his withering gaze was directed at Mr Swithin.

Mr Swithin swallowed drily.

"No," said Fred Brigstock. "Not Mr Ainsley."

"No, indeed," said Jane. "You owed money to Lord Herbert Longbottom which you weren't able to repay, despite his modest rates."

Fred Brigstock looked ill.

Jane continued. "The thing is, the Longbottoms had experienced their own downturn. That made it ripe for Mr Ainsley to apply some pressure on you." She turned to Desmond Ainsley specifically. "Is it fair to say you told Fred Brigstock you would buy his debt from Lord Longbottom?"

"I… don't recall."

"Mr Ainsley," said Jane, "you told Mr Brigstock that on acquiring his debt, you would take him to court for non-payment, which might mean him losing his farm to you."

"Nonsense," said Ainsley. "It was just a little fib to make Fred favour me, that's all. Lord Longbottom would never have sold the debt to me – hence, I never asked."

Fred Brigstock was aghast. "You lied!"

Desmond rolled his eyes. "Oh really, Fred. Grow up."

Jane cut in. "Was this what Lord Longbottom attempted to address, Mr Ainsley? Was he going to ask the police to look into your activities?"

"Not at all!" exclaimed Ainsley. "Honestly, Miles Longbottom is the one you should be questioning!"

Miles bristled. "How dare you!"

He looked to Jane for support, but none came.

"There *are* questions you can answer, Miles," she suggested.

"No, there are not!" he retorted.

Thirty-Six

Jane held Miles Longbottom's glare, which had the effect of making his heated response rebound on him.

"My apologies," he said. "I just don't see why I should be answering questions about my father's death."

"He telephoned you last Saturday, which might have been what put him in a concerned mood."

"His call was a minor family matter, nothing more."

"It had nothing to do with gambling debts then?"

The notion nudged Miles off course – but he recovered quickly.

"No, it did not."

"So, it wasn't about loans from sharks in London?"

"No."

Jane gave the faintest possible shrug.

"On Wednesday evening, you arrived at the town hall with a bruised face."

"Ha!" said Desmond Ainsley. "That definitely would've put Lord Longbottom in a bad mood."

Ignoring him, Miles kept his focus on Jane.

"As I've already stated, it was a minor injury caused by a cupboard door."

"Would you mind if I asked you about a painting then?"

Once again, Jane had wrongfooted Miles Longbottom.

"I'm not quite with you," he said.

"The trouble with rumours and gossip is once they're out there, the only way to disprove them is by unleashing the truth."

Miles laughed. "You mean all this public airing of private matters is for my own good?"

"Have you ever sold one of your father's paintings without his knowledge?"

But Miles was unshaken.

"Of course not. Why would I?"

"You mean there was no reason to plunder family heirlooms?"

"No."

"Because you have money?"

Ridley interjected. "Miles Longbottom works for Gladstone's, an investment broker in the City. I'm assuming the pay is good, but they're closed for the weekend and it's proving difficult to get anywhere – at least until Monday."

"The truth?" asked Jane.

"Miles has money," said Helen. "I'm sorry, Miles, but we cannot have a shadow over this house just for the sake of privacy. The fact is, Miles is far wealthier than our father ever was. He doesn't work for Gladstone's. He part-owns it."

Jane kept her gaze on the heir.

"So, who struck you?"

Miles took a moment then gave in.

"A loan shark. Well, two of the shark's heavies. Yes, I have money, but I stupidly threatened to see them in court. The thing is, they have false identities and use brutish go-betweens, and they certainly have no fear of our legal system, nor any use for it. They are their own law, and their punishments are severe. Once I realised that, I paid them off."

Jane raised an eyebrow.

"To be clear, this was your brother's debt."

All looked to Ian.

"Miles is setting me up in Brighton," he said somewhat sheepishly. "I've been a fool, but I won't let him down."

Helen rallied.

"Miles will make a wonderful head of this family. I'm very proud of him."

"You're right to be proud of him," said Jane. "The phone call last Saturday? Miles, I'm sure your father would have been pleased that you were sorting things out for your brother."

"Quite right," said Kate. "I can imagine him laughing when he heard of your misguided negotiations with the underworld."

"He did, Mrs Forbes." Miles smiled sadly at the memory.

"He would have seen you as a worthy heir."

"Thank you. I know he saw you as a true friend."

Kate flushed a little.

Meanwhile, Jane faced the wider gathering.

"Once this is over, I hope we can acknowledge that the incoming Lord Longbottom is a private man, which should be respected."

There was a general murmur of consent, while Miles gave the slightest of nods to Jane.

"So," declared Desmond Ainsley, "it was Patterson all along with a sly plan to implicate himself."

"No, it wasn't Mr Patterson," said Jane. "It was Mr Jenkins."

"Who?"

"Who indeed. Perhaps it's time we learned a little more about him."

"Ha!" said Perry Nash from behind Jane. "Mr Jenkins gave a false address. 72, Milburn Place on the outskirts of Brighton. When we arrived there, the line of houses ended at 70."

"Did you try the people at number 70?" asked Sir Christopher from the audience. "They might have known something."

Kate puffed out her cheeks. "Christopher, Mr Jenkins is unlikely to have introduced himself to the people at number 70 as a neighbour living in an invisible house next door to them."

"Ah…"

"It's alright," said Jane, "we clearly need some help with the mysterious Mr Jenkins. Perhaps you could assist us, Mr Royston?"

"Me?" gasped Guy Royston, the retort sticking in his throat.

Thirty-Seven

All eyes were now on Guy Royston, who was struggling to retain his usual air of quiet authority.

"The chief inspector has no interest in me," he pointed out. "I'm only here to discuss a memorial prize."

"All Saints is a wonderful school," said Jane, ignoring his explanation. "Can we presume it's a pleasure to work there?"

"A pleasure and a privilege," replied Guy.

"We know Lord Longbottom was in good spirits on Friday morning. We also know he was a troubled man before church on Sunday. Someone had clearly caused him a great deal of concern during that period. Thanks to my aunt, we know his lordship planned to speak to this person at the town hall."

"Yes – which rules me out," huffed Guy Royston.

"Yes, Headmaster. It's clear you never spoke to Lord Longbottom over the weekend. You were at your wife's sister's house in Eastbourne from Thursday until Sunday without a telephone."

"Exactly! I hadn't spoken with Herbert in ages."

"Are you sure?"

"Yes!" he insisted.

"The other thing I considered was the fire at the school."

"What's that got to do with anything?" he gasped.

"Five years ago, a fire in the school office destroyed furniture, records, invoices, receipts, and so on."

Hilda Royston leaned forward. "This is all wrong. My husband never started that fire."

"No, he didn't," said Jane. "We know how poor Mrs Trent caused it with her cigarette."

"Then why worry my wife and myself?" said Guy.

"Because of the goddess Venus," said Jane.

This caused a hubbub in the room.

"What?" groaned Guy.

"Don't you see?" said Jane.

"No, I do not. You're not fit to continue. Chief Inspector, stop her!"

Kate noted the worried looks, but Jane seemed confident.

"Yes, Venus," she said calmly. "And let's not forget Eric the toy engine."

"This is insane," raged Hilda. "Chief Inspector, please!"

Ridley looked a little uncertain but said nothing.

"It didn't come to me immediately," said Jane, "but my aunt reminded me of Sir Christopher Davenport's shock at his engine not being in the loft."

"A shock indeed," said Sir Christopher. "Thanks to my wife, my beloved Eric has spent the past ten years at the children's hospital in Brighton. Well, I had no idea."

"And Venus?" asked Helen.

"According to the Longbottom inventory," said Jane, "the statuette of Venus is somewhere in this house. Except it was damaged years ago by a young Miles and buried in the garden."

"Things that aren't where you'd expect them to be," mused Ian.

"Precisely," said Jane. "We spent time trying to learn who upset Lord Longbottom on Friday or Saturday – but this was never about *who*, it was about *what*."

"Which was…?" asked Ian.

Jane smiled. "Desmond Ainsley's newly acquired painting of a Tudor ship called Revenge."

Desmond sneered.

"Before you ask, I have a receipt for it!"

"Yes, you do," said Jane. "I confirmed it with the gallery. You told us Lord Longbottom admired your painting. He wasn't admiring it though; he was thinking he might have seen it before, many years ago, which is why he dug out the family inventory."

"I think I'm beginning to see," said Miles.

"Items in unexpected locations," said Jane. "While poor old Venus is at rest in the garden, and Eric is providing entertainment to children in Brighton, a third item, Revenge, is a Longbottom painting that's supposedly on loan to P."

"Who?" demanded Desmond Ainsley.

"P," repeated Jane. "That's why Lord Longbottom spoke to you, Mr Royston, about a painting on Wednesday evening at the town hall… and why he was due to visit the school at nine o'clock on Monday morning."

Thirty-Eight

Jane took a steadying breath.

"Lord Longbottom's suspicion that Revenge might be a painting his family had owned forty years ago proved correct. In fact, the family still own it but, all those years ago, Herbert's father loaned it to P."

"Who *is* P?" asked Ian Longbottom.

"Let's see," said Jane. "All Saints School's fortieth anniversary is almost upon us. It's a fine establishment with plenty going for it. It's a far cry from when it opened with not so much going for it. According to Sir Christopher, Lord Herbert Longbottom would occasionally tell of his father, Arthur, an early trustee at the school, seeking donations of everything from furniture to crockery, and loans of anything they could get their hands on."

"The school's early history is no secret," sighed Guy Royston.

"No, indeed, but years went by, the school gradually improved, and both Lady Rushton and Lord Arthur Longbottom passed away. Over a period of time, new custodians came in, standards continued to rise, new acquisitions were obtained, out-of-favour items supposedly belonging to Lady Rushton went into storage and became forgotten. The records were lost, and you, Guy Royston, saw a chance."

"Nonsense," he huffed.

"It probably never occurred to you right away," said Jane, "but it became apparent that your gift to the next headmaster might be a spotless new inventory of everything in the school. As for the items in storage though – well, no need to record those if you sold them off for cash and kept the money for yourself. After all, who would know? Not Mrs Trent, that's for sure. She never returned to the school after the fire. And it was several months before a new office assistant was appointed. Your wife held the fort between times."

"My wife has worked tirelessly. You cannot taint her with lies."

"You found paintings. How many? Only you know – at least until a police investigation finds out. You supposed all these old treasures must have belonged to Lady Rushton."

"You've proved nothing."

"The fact is, Mr Royston, you told my aunt you were retiring soon and painted a rosy picture of it. However, your retirement income would perhaps be too limiting for a man who's spent a quarter of a century living in ever more opulent surroundings while mixing with ever higher echelons of society, including the grandest nobility and foreign royals."

Guy Royston merely shook his head, so Jane continued.

"Posing as Mr Jenkins, you sold paintings for your own benefit."

"No."

"You probably left it for a time to see if anything would happen. Had any questions been raised, you would've declared an oversight and that the items were safe in the storeroom. No harm done. They could now be added to the new inventory. But no questions were raised."

Guy Royston shook his head again.

"I'd guess you chose a variety of places to sell them," said Jane. "Maybe you gave the dealers a story – an impoverished lord who wished to remain incognito, or perhaps you spun a sorry tale of your own. Paintings with a lack of provenance might mean a lower price, but to you it was pure profit."

Guy Royston sighed heavily, indicating his displeasure.

Jane continued. "It worked perfectly until Lord Longbottom asked for a painting his father had loaned to the school."

"I really don't know what you're talking about."

"Oh, but it must have come as a shock to learn that Revenge had never belonged to Lady Rushton."

"Honestly, all this was long before my time."

"Lord Longbottom's school visits were generally social events. Making an appointment to visit you at nine o'clock on a Monday morning was very unlike him. It must have been important. It also means he spoke to you before Wednesday's town hall function in order to make that appointment. Most likely, a telephone call. It can easily be checked with Miss Evans at the school."

"Yes, alright, I may have spoken with him…"

"Yes, and Lord Longbottom had seen in the family inventory that Revenge was on loan to P."

"Really," said Guy Royston, "you can't link this mythical P to the school."

"No? The only other possibility would be Robert Patterson's paternal grandfather serving in the army alongside Lord Arthur Longbottom."

This caused a gasp.

"Well, there you are then. P for Patterson!"

"Yes… except it doesn't make sense. Why loan a painting to a fellow officer? No, this morning in Brighton, my aunt mentioned her friend, Ginny."

"Not more rot…"

"You see, Herbert recalled P from his younger days. It was a lady his father helped – Margaret, the daughter of Lord Shepton and wife of Sir Owen Rushton."

"Ah…" said Pru, "P is Lady Rushton."

Jane nodded. "While Ginny is short for Virginia, Peggy is a popular way to shorten Margaret. Perhaps Revenge originally decorated the school's entrance hall. Possibly, as the school began to do well, it was relegated to a corridor or the dining room. Sometime after Lady Rushton and Lord Arthur Longbottom passed away, it found its way into the storeroom. Perhaps it was deemed out of vogue. Who knows."

"This is all speculation," said Guy Royston. "Nothing more."

Jane continued. "When Lord Herbert Longbottom asked to see Revenge, your heart must have hit the floor. You had already sold it. Legally, it should have been in the new school inventory as an owned and then sold painting, but that document won't show it. If it did, there would be no problem. You could have apologised to Lord Longbottom for selling it, citing old records destroyed in the fire. But this was not possible."

Guy Royston folded his arms. He wasn't impressed.

"There was no way out of it," continued Jane. "Had you falsely logged ownership of the painting and its sale in the school's records a few days ago, Miss Evans might have seen it. You could have fired her, but that would have made Lord Longbottom even more suspicious. Certainly, he might have asked to see the paperwork relating to the sale, or asked his friend the bank manager about it, as that's where the school banks. Or possibly, he'd ask his friend Sir Ronald Hope, the Chief Constable of Sussex for advice. Then there's Desmond Ainsley who purchased Revenge from the Grosvenor Gallery, who themselves had bought it with another painting from Mr Jenkins for cash. How could you explain it? The game would be up."

Guy Royston unfolded his arms.

"Complete nonsense."

"You must have been under tremendous pressure," said Jane. "You could have said it had been stolen or gone missing, or any other excuse, but Lord Longbottom would have called in the police, who might have suspected this fictitious Mr Jenkins selling paintings to be yourself. What if the gallery owner remembered you? What if the other painting you sold along with Revenge could be traced back to Lady Rushton? What if Lady Rushton's private papers survived in an archive somewhere, now to be examined? The likelihood of spending your retirement in prison was growing fast… and you weren't prepared to countenance such an appalling end to an illustrious career. Therefore, you could not go ahead with the Monday morning meeting. In short, Lord Longbottom had to be silenced."

Thirty-Nine

Guy Royston slowly shook his head. For a moment, Kate thought he was about to break into laughter, but he composed himself and spoke calmly.

"This… is the ramblings… of an amateur."

"Yes," said Ridley, "but a rather good amateur. For example, it was Lady Jane Scott who discovered that the invitation card sent to Robert Patterson was a clever forgery."

A large portion of the gathering gasped as one.

"Mr Patterson's invitation arrived at the last minute," continued Ridley, "making sure he didn't have time to think about it. Of course, it was a prestigious event, so he was bound to turn up, just as you planned, Mr Royston. In fact, my inquiries place you at the main entrance to make sure that the doorman, Ernie Melton, had no reason to check his invitation too closely."

"No, this is nonsense."

"Distraction was your method. That meant working closely with Mrs Royston to engage Lord Longbottom, swap an already poisoned glass with his, and place a small, slim bottle into the jacket pocket of an innocent man."

"No."

"I expect you practised at home. I know I would."

Ridley signalled to Edmonds, who nodded and showed in the two people who had been in the back of the police car – Robert Patterson and his mother.

"Please take a seat," said Pru as she and Sir Christopher rose to make way.

The new arrivals thanked them and duly sat.

Ridley then nodded to Jane.

"Mrs Royston," she said, "you and your husband sold paintings to improve your situation in retirement. And yet, the arrival of Lord Longbottom at the school on Monday at nine o'clock was likely to end up with the police being called and the pair of you going to prison. You had just a few days to do something about it."

To say the least, Mrs Royston looked uncomfortable.

"You no doubt had cyanide in the gardening shed – it's common enough for killing weeds. There was also an event at the town hall that his lordship would attend – an event to which you and your husband were invited, making it a straightforward business for you to make a copy of your card and send it to Mr Patterson, who you clearly knew had a history with Lord Longbottom from their army days. It was an opportunity to silence a lord and let Mr Patterson hang for it. Your plan, in effect, was designed to cause his poor mother the utmost personal torture and distress."

While Jane was indicating the victims, Mrs Royston shook her head and mouthed, "No..."

"You relished the prospect of this young man's life ending on the gallows because it would mean a successful conclusion to your plan."

"No..."

"Look at them sitting there, mother and son. It takes a brutal, hardened, soulless devil to take pleasure in such injustices."

"No..."

"Did you plan to celebrate with champagne?"

"No!"

"Was it hard to persuade your husband to help you?"

"Me?" gasped Mrs Royston.

"You are pure evil."

"No!"

"A champagne cork popping and a neck snapping!"

"No!"

"Fizz in your mouth and gasping death in your head?"

"No! I said murder was too much!"

"Be quiet!" hissed Guy Royston.

"No... I was against the idea!"

"Hilda, stop."

And Mrs Royston did stop. But only for a moment.

Then she began again, in a softer voice.

"We built the school's reputation for no reward. For us, it's nothing more than a luxurious prison. Almost nothing of it is ours. All those years…"

She took a moment to compose herself further, while her husband looked on, crestfallen.

"We lived with the trappings of wealth," she continued, "dealing with parents who were lords and ladies, and foreign royalty… and yet, retirement loomed, waiting to cast us back into the ordinary world on meagre rations."

"You decided you deserved more," said Jane.

"Not at first. We worked on the new inventory with no ulterior motive. Then, one afternoon, all we had left to check was the storeroom. We knew there was old junk down there, but we were surprised to find more than a dozen paintings at the back, gathering dust."

"I vaguely remembered them being there before the War," said Guy. By now, he seemed resigned to his fate. "I assumed they were Lady Rushton's possessions and that they had long ago fallen out of favour and been forgotten. So, we left them off the new inventory and waited a couple of years. Then, when no one asked, we sold one in Chichester for cash."

"We hid the money in a sock," said Hilda. "Six months later, we sold another. And so on. Revenge was one of the final two."

"Then Lord Longbottom asked about it," lamented Mr Royston. "Right away, I telephoned the gallery anonymously to see if I could buy it, but it had already been sold. The dealer refused to name the buyer."

"Yes, unfortunately for you, it was Desmond Ainsley, who was keen to show off his bargain to visitors."

Sir Christopher stirred. "Knowing Ainsley, he'd have sold it to you as long as he made a profit."

"How dare you!" growled Desmond Ainsley.

"It was the perfect plan," said Jane. "On your retirement, a new headmaster would check the inventory, which would be perfectly in order."

"It was nothing personal," said Guy Royston. "We liked Lord Longbottom."

"And what about Robert Patterson?"

Guy looked more uncomfortable.

"I was at a drinks thing with Lord Longbottom when Mr Patterson returned to Sandham. Herbert described it as a potentially tricky situation and wondered how to handle it. I suggested they keep out of each other's way and that nothing need be said."

"But it gave you the idea of a grudge."

Mr Royston shrugged.

"Why not just pay the money back?" said Miles.

"If only! We could have lied it was being set aside for the Longbottom Gym or something and all would have been forgiven."

"But we'd already spent it," said Mrs Royston. "Every penny went on a lovely cottage with grounds in South Devon. Trying to sell it immediately was impossible."

Guy sighed. "We thought of raising a private loan just to cover what we owed Lord Longbottom, but we had so many fears. What if he asked to see the inventory, or the receipt book, or the docket from the dealer, or what if he spoke to the dealer, or what if we'd triggered his own memories of other paintings? We had no idea what he knew or didn't know. There were just all these endless avenues to having the police called in. How would we keep everything covered up? It was a nightmare…"

"You were stuck then," said Jane, "with only one way out."

Mr and Mrs Royston both nodded apologetically.

"Guy Royston, Hilda Royston," proclaimed Ridley, "I'm arresting you both for the murder of Lord Herbert Longbottom…"

A few moments later, Kate and Jane followed the chief inspector outside to the driveway, where Edmonds was helping the culprits into the police car.

"Do you know something?" said Kate. "I almost feel sorry for them."

Ridley shrugged. "That's because you're a decent person. The fact is when temptation came their way, they didn't fight it."

"Yes, well, temptation likes to test us, doesn't it. With me, it's sponge cake."

"Hardly a job for Scotland Yard, Mrs Forbes."

"No, thankfully. Well, we wish you well, Chief Inspector. And congratulations once again on your promotion."

"It was a pleasure to assist you," said Jane.

Ridley nodded. "For your own peace of mind, let's hope the need to assist me doesn't arise again. If it does though, let me just say that, unofficially, I'll be very happy to have you alongside. Good day, Mrs Forbes… Lady Jane."

They watched him get in the car. A few moments later, Chief Inspector Leonard Ridley was disappearing out of view. Come Monday, he would be back at Scotland Yard ready to face whatever challenge came his way next.

As for Kate Forbes, it was thoughts of a nice cup of tea and a slice of cake that had begun to take precedence. That, and one other thing.

"It's shame Desmond Ainsley didn't get his comeuppance, Jane," she said.

For some reason, Jane's response was to smile mischievously.

"That's still to come, Aunt."

Forty

Kate and Jane returned to a general hubbub in the grand salon. On one side, Perry and the Pattersons were with Pru and Sir Christopher, listening to the latter's theory on some aspect of the case. On the other side, Fred Brigstock was talking with Mr Swithin and the vicar and his wife. Between these two groups, Helen and Ian Longbottom were also in conversation.

It was Miles Longbottom who came over to Kate and Jane by the door.

"Well, I don't wish to go through any of that again," he puffed.

"No, indeed," said Kate.

"We're sorry to have disrupted your meeting," said Jane.

Miles gave a little laugh.

"My father would have loved it."

Just then Helen and Ian came to join them.

"Thank you," said Helen. "People will always gossip, but any news leaving this house today should persuade them that Miles acted properly in steering Ian towards a more responsible and stable life."

Ian shrugged. "It's for the best."

"I'm glad to hear it," said Kate. She turned to Miles. "Um… I'm hoping the Sandham campaign is still on?"

"I'll be backing Sandham all the way," he confirmed.

Miles then thanked them again before he, Ian and Helen withdrew to talk with the Davenports, the Pattersons, and Perry. At this, Desmond Ainsley stepped in.

"I've decided to make a gesture," he told Kate and Jane.

"Oh really?" Kate was surprised.

"It's the reason I was here today. The lane that leads up to the Ridgeway development. I've decided to name it Herbert Longbottom Drive."

"That's very magnanimous, Mr Ainsley," said Kate, knowing it to be Fred Brigstock's idea.

"It's the least I can do. Herbert and I shared a passion for integrity and honesty."

"About those houses…" said Jane.

"Yes?" said Desmond with a glimmer of annoyance in his eyes.

"You knew Simon Townsend's deal with Fred Brigstock would make Simon a decent profit. The problem was he couldn't pay Fred until all the houses were built and sold."

"Honestly, ladies, it's all settled."

"Fred's fortunes haven't been good over recent years," continued Jane. "The farm was making a loss and he needed money urgently for animal feed and workers' wages. You lied and took advantage."

"A misunderstanding, that's all."

"Simon had done all the work," said Kate. "He'd sought permission from Fred, worked out the best piece of land to build on, had estimates drawn up, consulted a drainage expert, talked to the telephone and water people… then you muscled in. Lord Longbottom was looking into it because he hated seeing sharp practice in Sandham."

"If you've finished…?"

Jane smiled. "I hear your daughter's marrying into the Faulkner-Smythe family."

Desmond seemed unsettled.

"What of it?"

"Oh, it's just that I'm thinking of popping over to see Lady Faulkner-Smythe next week. I can't wait to tell her all the exciting news about Mr Desmond Ainsley and his property shenanigans."

Desmond baulked.

"You can't tell her that. She'll think I'm a crook!"

"Hand the housebuilding deal back to Simon Townsend."

"What?"

"I said hand it back," insisted Jane.

"This is nothing short of intimidation."

"Let's be frank. Lady Faulkner-Smythe is a bigger snob than you. I'm sure she wouldn't want her son marrying your daughter *if* she found out."

Ainsley's eyes narrowed.

"Jane Scott, you're no lady!"

"And you'll hand Revenge over to Miles without a challenge – as a gesture to your dear old friend, Herbert."

The money lender resembled a cobra, ready to strike... but instead, he smiled thinly.

"Do you know something – I'm leaving Sandham. I've decided it's too small for me. A man of vision needs a bigger stage."

"Oh?"

"Brighton! I have in fact already bought a property there."

Kate sighed. *Poor Brighton.*

Desmond Ainsley then placed a very fine cigar in his mouth and headed out to his Rolls-Royce motorcar muttering something about life being incredibly unfair for some.

"Mrs Forbes?"

Kate turned to find Robert Patterson and his mother smiling at her and Jane.

"We owe you everything," said Mrs Patterson.

"Nonsense," said Kate. "Jane and I were only too happy to lend a hand."

"Well, thank you from both of us," said Robert.

"Yes, thank you," echoed his mother.

"You're both very welcome," said Jane.

Robert appeared to have something else on his mind.

"Mrs Forbes… your idea for a visitor information service."

"Yes?"

"Well, if you can obtain some office space that the public can easily find, then that would be marvellous."

"Alas, it's proving difficult. There seems to be no shortage of back rooms, cellars and lofts miles from anywhere. As for being in the thick of the action though…"

"In that case, I might have a solution."

"Oh?"

"You'll need to persuade the powers-that-be to grant you a small space on the quayside first."

"For what reason?"

"If you can acquire the space, I'll build you a nice roomy kiosk at no charge to yourself or the town."

"Really?"

"It would be lockable with a door at the side and a fully opening window for dispensing information to passing visitors."

Kate's heart swelled. It was a marvellous idea. And the town council and Harbour Board would have no reason to be against it.

"I can see it now," she enthused. "Volunteers could sell tickets for boat trips and offer advice and leaflets to visitors to improve their stay."

"You like the idea then?"

"What can I say, Robert. Thank you very much. You're a credit to Sandham."

Robert Patterson beamed somewhat bashfully, while his mum's smile told of her pride and joy.

Forty-One

As the Sunday morning service at St Matthew's Church ended, Kate and Jane rose from their seats along with Perry Nash, who had booked into the Crown Hotel for a couple of days.

Kate took a moment to look around the airy nave. It was such a lovely setting – fringed with decorated columns that supported the roof, while beyond the altar, light streamed in through a lovely stained glass main window.

"I'll be outside," said Jane, diplomatically leaving the scene.

"A lovely service," said Perry. "Mr and Mrs Brigstock looked happy."

"Yes, they did," agreed Kate.

With Simon Townsend back in charge, the Brigstocks would earn enough to pay back the Longbottoms at Miles' new generous rate of nought percent interest.

Remaining where they stood, Kate and Perry were soon alone.

"Perry, I don't want to rush into anything. If that disappoints you, I'll understand."

But Perry could only smile.

"Kate, you're right. You must be certain of what you want. But... you *do* agree we have a chance of being together?"

"I do." It then struck Kate she'd just uttered the words she hoped to utter again in different circumstances.

"Then let me put your mind at ease," said Perry. "I'll be here when you're ready. Er... I mean *here* in the abstract sense, not standing on this exact spot."

Kate laughed and felt the warmth of his words.

"Right then," she said, "we'd better leave before the vicar hauls us to the altar."

Outside, they joined Jane on the patch of green between the church and the lychgate. For a moment, Kate looked across the lane to the bench by the pond. She would return in the week and sit there to feed the ducks – because opportunities to enjoy the simple life were far too often overlooked.

*

To work up an appetite for lunch, Kate, Jane and Perry strolled through the huddle of tight, narrow, 18th and early 19th century lanes that led down to the Sandham Harbour quayside.

Once there, Kate peered across the water to the tiny hamlet of Holton. One day, boats trips from Sandham would take visitors there for nature walks and picnics.

This gave her pause for thought. Where would the Visitor Information kiosk stand?

"Fishermen," said Perry, indicating a couple of men with pole rods about sixty feet away. "I've fished many a river and lake, but never salt water. I wonder what they catch here?"

"Why don't you ask," said Kate. "I'm sure they'd be only too happy to advise a fellow enthusiast."

"Good idea."

They watched him go off to join the local fishermen for a chat.

"Well," puffed Kate. "It's been quite a week."

"Yes, it has, Aunt."

"You know, Sandham is quite the place. I know it's had one or two hiccups recently, but I feel we have something visitors will love for years to come."

"I agree, and you're in a good position to make sure everyone is pulling in the same direction. You should definitely be on the town council."

Kate let the idea sit there for a moment.

"Perhaps."

She watched Perry. He was pointing to one end of the harbour while the chap with him pointed the other way.

"Did you speak to him?" asked Jane.

"Yes, I did. I explained my situation and he said he would happily wait until I'm ready to take the next step."

"That's what I expected."

Kate studied Professor Peregrine Nash, who seemed to be receiving a lecture on the local waters. What would happen between them? Would they really tie the matrimonial knot?

"You know, Jane, one day, if I were…"

"…married?"

Kate laughed. "Yes, that. And not just me, but you too. I just thought… well, hoped really…"

"That we'd remain steadfast friends regardless?"

"Yes."

"That we'd see each other often?"

"Yes."

"That we'd tackle any mystery that came our way as a team?"

"It's what I've been wondering."

"Me too, Aunt. It's my hope that we'll stick together like two peas in a pod come what may."

"It's mine too."

"Then, come what may, let there be no stopping us."

"You know, I like the sound of that."

Aunt and niece shared a smile.

"Jane, it's a shame we can't say the same for working with Chief Inspector Ridley. The chances must be quite slim."

"I wouldn't be so sure, Aunt. Our reputation is spreading, and people are always in need of someone to turn to. It's just a guess, but I think in helping others, ours and the chief inspector's paths might well cross again."

Kate nodded with satisfaction at the prospect. Into her fifties, life was unexpectedly moving in a new direction. Having feared loneliness and insignificance, she was now embracing companionship and potentially quite a bit more. There were other avenues too – not least of all, her work to promote Sandham and perhaps the occasional foray into the realm of the amateur sleuth.

All in all, things were chugging along quite nicely.

Long may it continue, thought Mrs Kate Forbes.

The End (Until Next Time…)

Thank you for reading 'The Unfortunate Death of Lord Longbottom'.

Don't miss the next book in the series.
For details, please visit our website.

www.churstonmysteries.com

Printed in Great Britain
by Amazon